CANDLELIGHT GEORGIAN SPECIAL

CANDLELIGHT REGENCIES

RESCUED BY LOVE

Joan Vincent

A CANDLELIGHT GEORGIAN SPECIAL

to Jennifer, Will, and Kathryn

Published by
Dell Publishing Co., Inc.
1 Dag Hammarskjold Plaza
New York, New York 10017

Dell ® TM 681510, Dell Publishing Co., Inc.

ISBN: 0-440-17433-3

Printed in the United States of America

First printing—January 1981

Chapter I

The beauty of the Sussex countryside in this summer of 1803 was momentarily forgotten by the three travelers as they were jounced over a particularly bad section of back-country road which had not been improved by a recent drenching.

" 'Twas vastly unreasonable for us not to recall circumstances such as this," spritely, white-haired Lady Phillippa, Dowager Marchioness of Bawden, noted as she righted herself, only to be thrown forward by another sudden lurch of the coach.

"I do think we may have gone too bloody far in deciding to use the same coach we did in 'fifty-nine," the Dowager Countess of Lackland, Lady Imogene, declared, holding onto the strap beside her. Her buxom figure swayed violently at each jolt. "My Berlin is so much better sprung. Perhaps we should relent on having things exactly as they were. We could find a comfortable inn and send for it," she offered, her pink cheeks dimpling hopefully as a gray curl tumbled free from its pin and dangled across her forehead. A gasp escaped as the coach lurched to a sudden halt amid the shouts and urgings of the coachman.

Seemingly unaffected by the constant jostling, the thin form of the Dowager Baroness of Mickle, Lady Brienne, relaxed as she waved a gloved hand non-

chalantly. "My dears, all you have done since we began this journey is grieve at the alterations we
have met with—the disappearance of that little inn
just beyond Dover, the absence of the Culvers from
Ashford. I would think you would rejoice that at
least one item remains unchanged—the roads are as
ghastly as they were on our first journey." Inwardly
the stiff old woman sighed. *Why did I ever agree to
come with them?* she questioned herself. A tear
pricked her eye, for the baroness knew that she had
consented in the hope of recapturing a gleam of the
happiness she had shared with her husband, her dear
Robert, dead these four years past. Anger welled as it
always did when she thought of his loss, and her
scowl deepened.

Lady Imogene and Lady Phillippa cast suspicious
glances at their eldest sister. Over sixty years in her
company had taught them to be wary of her haugh-
tier moods.

The flush-faced coachman opened the door after a
thumping knock. Sweat flowed freely from his brow,
and his too-tight jacket had lost three of its buttons in
his exertions. "Miladies, 'tis nothing can be done. We
must seek aid."

"What has happened?" Lady Phillippa popped her
head out the window to inspect the surroundings.
"Butterflies and blueberries!" she exclaimed. "We are
adrift in a sea of mud."

"Adrift is not the word, milady. This coach will
go no further this day." The coachman mopped his
brow.

"Caine, that is impossible. Surely you can do something," the baroness said, leaning forward stiffly to

6

peer at the brown-pooled morass surrounding them.

"'Tis sadly true, milady," the coachman's head bobbed. "Not only do we suffer a surfeit of muck, but that last rut splintered the rear axle as well. The cattle cannot draw the coach forward."

"What is your intent?" Lady Brienne demanded, her head cocked challengingly.

"With your ladyships' permission, me and Ben will walk to the next village and return with a carriage for you. Methinks 'twill be a day, nay longer, to mend the damage done, once we free the coach."

"And what will you have us do while you accomplish this?" the baroness demanded, her parasol indenting Caine's corpulent stomach.

"Why, milady, you . . . you do as you wish." Attempting to retreat from her jabbing, the unfortunate man lost his balance. Flailing his arms wildly, he sat down heavily, causing a great splash of mud and water.

"Now look what you've done, Brienne," the countess admonished. "Are you quite all right, Mr. Caine?"

"Yes, milady. 'Haps Ben and Josh should help you to the grass?" the coachman asked, looking gratefully at the concerned face peering down at him.

"Oh, there is some delightful shade just beyond the road," Marchioness Bawden's voice piped. "I recommend you join me there, sisters dear."

"Phillippa," gasped Lady Brienne, a sound echoed faintly by Lady Imogene. "Four and forty years have not altered you one twit. Cover your ankles before you scandalize all."

Ignoring the scold, the marchioness cupped her shoes and hose in her uplifted skirts and moved to

7

the coach's steps. "If you will assist me, Mr. Caine, with the cleaner hand," she cautioned as he struggled upright, using one hand to raise his heavy frame from the muck.

"Milady," he bowed and offered the recommended hand.

"Come, Brienne . . . Imogene. The mire is quite cooling," Lady Phillippa called as she stepped lightly to the edge of the quagmire.

"You wouldn't," Lady Brienne censored the countess, as she undid the lacing of her shoes.

"Oh, come, Brienne. What else are we to do?"

"Recall your age for one matter, and your station in life for another," she admonished.

"Neither my age nor my station advocate an afternoon in a stuffy, overly warm, highly uncomfortable coach," Lady Imogene returned, her shoes off. "I haven't felt the squish of mud through my toes since I was . . . well, younger."

"At four and sixty she speaks of 'younger.' " The baroness shook her head sadly.

"What has been troubling you, Brienne? One would think you are six and ten years older than I, instead of a mere five. You know you want to come with us," she cajoled gently. "No one will see you. Why, we haven't met but one carriage all day."

"The servants . . ."

"Davey Caine has been with the family for seven and forty years and is well accustomed to your unusual ways. We've known his sons, Ben and Josh, since their births. Servants? Folderol, my lady. Swelter if you must. Yon tree's gentle shade is too inviting for me to resist," the countess returned a rare challenge.

Coachman Caine had returned to the coach's door and took Lady Imogene's plump arm as she stepped down.

"Imogene, come along," Lady Phillippa called. "There is a stream here where you can wash your feet and refresh yourself."

The baroness watched her sister's ample figure, skirts hoisted clear of the mire, as she waddled to the edge of the morass. A beseeching backward glance did not soften her resolve.

"Milady?" Caine asked, returning to the door.

"I shall remain here," Lady Brienne told him curtly.

"Me and Ben will hurry, milady."

"Then be off instead of babbling about it," she scolded, sitting rigidly. The stiffness left as she sank against the cushions when the coachman turned away. *Now why did you do that,* she reprimanded herself. *You are becoming a snapping, old . . .* Her thoughts drifted melancholily. Phillippa's bright laughter, undimmed even at one and sixty, sounded clearly, followed by Imogene's deeper peal, as full of life as her ample form. "Bedlamites. Foolish old women. Why do they refuse to act their age?" the baroness snapped angrily. She closed her eyes, listening to Caine and his sons as they unhooked the teams and led them clear of the mud. There was a further jangle of harness as one pair was freed for the ride to the next village. When all became still, Lady Brienne peered out the window. "Josh," she called, "Josh, where are you?"

"Here, milady." The awkward lad left the remaining team's side and trudged to the coach.

"Tether the cattle so they will remain in the shade as the day passes. Then walk a furlong down the road and keep watch for brigands. I do not wish to be taken unawares."

"But what if they come from before us, milady? Wouldn't it be best if I stay close?" Josh rubbed a hand through his hair.

"Do as I command at once."

"Yes, milady," he bowed, still hesitant.

The baroness glared until he turned away, then leaned back, regretting her harshness. *Josh had not even been born when we first made this journey,* she thought. That was so long ago and yet so like yesterday. A smile softened the baroness's features as memories surged. Little had they realized what it would mean for them on that fated day four and forty years past, when the letter had arrived telling of their uncle's death and his bequest of a sum of money for an "educational tour of England" for his brother's daughters. Their father had reluctantly consented to his three eldest making use of the bequest and carefully plotted a course, which included all major and many minor historical sites, and a fair sampling of every variety of English countryside. Little did he guess that before their journey ended each of his daughters would be engaged or wed to a titled lord. A chuckle escaped Lady Brienne as she thought of the madcap adventures they had shared . . . and of Robert, her dear love. Shaking herself, she looked out the window at the verdant scene. Their father had valued it as an example of England's southeastern beauty, and, reluctantly, she admitted that the years had not altered it.

With a shrug Lady Brienne deftly untied her shoelaces, removed her shoes, and plucked off her hose. Warily she arose and checked both fore and aft of the coach before stepping into the mire. Her sisters' voices a guide, the baroness strode through the morass as if walking down St. James's and did not halt until she reached the stream where they sat.

"How glad I am you relented," Lady Phillippa greeted her eagerly. "Oh, do loosen your stays, Brenny."

"I wear no such garment," the other returned caustically.

"We know that. Philly meant you are taking this 'dignity of age' too bloody serious," Lady Imogene tossed in irreverently.

"We shall be ever youthful," the marchioness laughed, and splashed spiritedly into the water. "Join us, Brienne. The water is so cool. But do watch for the sharp stones."

She frowned and stepped gingerly forward.

Josh, asleep in a soft bed of honey clover, awoke to a sweet, lilting voice. His thought that he had left this world was erased by the bothersome lump beneath his back. Raising his head slowly, he saw a waif-sized maid sauntering down the road lost in song and thought. A mighty shrug heaved his large form from the clover with a suddenness that stilled the words upon her lips, halted her steps, and blanched the healthy glow from her cheeks.

"Do not fear, miss," Josh stammered, realizing his abrupt appearance had frightened her.

"You are a stranger. What is your purpose?" the maid's brave voice trembled.

"My name is Josh Caine and miladies' coach has met with a mishap. You can see it . . . there, yon." He drew himself up proudly as he pointed.

"I will do no harm to your mistresses." Her colour slowly returned. "Is it not an odd road for you to travel? Do you go to visit Lord Pergrine?"

"Oh, no, miss. Their ladyships are remaking a journey they took many years past. I do not think they know of a Lord Per . . ."

"Pergrine," she ended for him with a kind smile. "Have you been here long?"

"Since late morn." Josh rubbed his stomach and looking to the west. "I wonder what is keeping me dad. He's our driver," he explained. "And the ladies. I had best see how they fare." He turned to go to the coach.

"Have none of you eaten since this morn?"

"No, miss. But I'll wager their ladyships have something tasty in the baskets we stowed earlier." His eyes brightened at the thought. "Lady Imogene does wonders with the plainest picnique fare."

"Lady Imogene . . . Your mistress is titled?" the petite miss asked, trying to match her steps to Josh's strides.

"Why, yes, miss. They are all titled, and the best of mistresses. They be fair 'n just 'n generous—a baroness, a countess, and a marchioness. Most folks call them the dowagers," he added, encouraged by his companion's respectful awe. The young lad went on to explain how the widowed sisters had visited together oft after their husbands' deaths, and how they were now traveling on the same route they had taken when they were scarcely out of their teens.

"When was the original journey made?" she asked, her curiosity tweaked by his descriptions of the three and his apparent familiarity with them.

"Far back in seventeen fifty-nine. I know 'cause they've been speakin' so much about it with all the plannin' . . ." Josh's voice trailed off as he halted near the coach. "Where could they have gone? And me dad, he be uncommon late. Would you be knowin' how far the next village is, miss?"

"Miss Durham," the firm voice told him. "What was his direction?" A frown came as Josh pointed up the road. "Along that way it would be over a half day's ride. I fear your father will not return until late." Concern had entered her voice.

"I best find their ladyships. Me dad says you never know what they might take in mind to do."

"But how did they manage the mud? 'Tis ghastly thick and deep," Miss Durham noted, studying the coach's position.

"Lady Phillippa, that's the Marchioness of Bawden, she . . . well." He blushed, thinking of what he had heard the baroness say. Not wishing to embarrass his mistresses, he shrugged, his eyes seeking the ground at his feet.

"Josh, there you are. We were about to search for you." Lady Imogene halted and took in the petite miss beside the footman. "We heard no other coach," she began.

"I am Sarita Durham, daughter of Reverend Durham of Braitlathe," the young woman offered, stepping forward.

"Miss says me dad won't be comin' back till late, milady," Josh interposed.

"Oh, dear. How dreadful." The countess's full-cheeked face sagged into a frown. "Brienne will be . . . But how did you come here, Miss Durham?" she asked, realizing that neither cart, carriage, nor pony was to be seen.

"I called upon the Culvers and Laithes today, and this is my usual way home," Sarita responded matter-of-factly.

"Walking alone? My, such a little thing as you alone," Lady Imogene clucked.

"My sister usually accompanies me, but Mother had need of her. There is none to harm me."

"Have you not heard of Napoleon's plan to attack us?"

"Imogene . . . Whom do we have here?" the baroness asked, seeing Miss Durham with her sister.

"Reverend Durham's daughter," the countess replied as if a long acquaintance existed. "Miss Durham, my sister, Lady Brienne, Baroness Mickle," she offered by way of introduction.

"The dowager baroness," Lady Brienne corrected. "Why do you refuse to be correct, Imogene? After all, you are the Dowager Countess of Lackland."

Lady Imogene's face wrinkled in irritation, which changed to distress as she recalled Sarita's words. She hurried to impart them to Brienne.

Watching the two women, a smile played upon the rector's daughter's face. The sisters were as unalike as strangers, the thin, stern form of the one forming a counterpart to the full, buxom figure of the other.

"Now, why are you standing about?" Lady Phillippa's light voice challenged as she joined her sisters.

"Why, what a lovely young girl you are, my dear," she noted, seeing Miss Durham.

All three inspected the diminutive figure of the young miss with her slender form and pert face. Her bright, dark eyes returned gaze for gaze.

What an odd assortment, Miss Durham thought, taking in the dowagers' old-fashioned, once-elegant traveling gowns. For all their titles, she thought, their husbands must have left them with depleted funds for them to band together and travel in such an ancient coach.

The openness of Miss Durham's face and the pride apparent in her stance met with their approval. After a brief, whispered conference, Lady Brienne turned to Sarita. "Being of the area, could you direct us to a nearby inn where we can take lodgings until our coach is repaired?"

Dismay touched the spritely miss's features. "There is none, not unless you go back to Runnet or ahead to Pordean. Both are much too far for you to attempt to walk."

"Surely a village is close by. Your home?" Lady Imogene asked.

Sarita laughed lightly. "There is no village, only Father's church and the rectory. But there is . . ." She took in the ladies, weighed the reception Lord Pergrine would give them in such worn garments, and tossed the idea aside. "You are welcome to come to the rectory," Miss Durham ended, her fingers crossed in the folds of her skirt. "It is not too distant," she added, "and would be far more comfortable for you than remaining here."

"Oh, yes, Brienne. Let us go," urged the countess.

"It would be most interesting," added Lady Phillippa, seeing, as always, an adventure before them.

"I assure you that the rectory is neither small nor overrun with children," Sarita told Lady Brienne, guessing her thoughts. "It is unusually large, in fact, singular as a rectory." Her mind flew over the possibilities of the garden. "And there may be enough ripe strawberries for tarts."

"Oh, we must go," said Lady Imogene. "Lead the way, Miss Durham. Josh, you fetch the horses along," she ordered.

"You do have space for them?" Lady Phillippa questioned.

"Something will be managed, my lady," Sarita told her with a smile. "Shouldn't you leave a message for your coachman?"

"Caine knows us too well to worry. We shall send Josh back later with a note. For now, let us go," Lady Brienne told her. "Josh, you get the baskets from the coach and bring them along," she ordered. If Miss Durham can extend her hospitality, we can contribute our own resources, she thought, grudgingly approving of Imogene's impetuous acceptance of the young woman's invitation. From the worn gown she wears, our breads, cheeses, wines, and fruits will be a welcome addition to their larder, she decided.

"You must tell us about your family, Miss Durham," Lady Phillippa said eagerly. "Have you other than a sister? Surely there are some families living nearby? Why would your father have a church if there were not?"

As their questions continued, the marchioness took Miss Durham's arm and beckoned her to lead on.

Lady Imogene followed closely, with Josh coming after them leading the team, the heavy baskets tied to their harness. Only the baroness hesitated. Pressing her lips into a tight frown, she strode forward.

The marchioness motioned Lady Imogene to Miss Durham's side and joined Lady Brienne. "Isn't Miss Durham a lovely, tiny thing?" she whispered. "I wonder if she is betrothed?"

Lady Brienne threw a cautioning, warning glance at her sister.

"Well, I was only wondering. After all, what would our trip be if we did not assist at least one romance after encountering our own on this same journey so many years ago?"

Chapter II

Two furlongs up the road Sarita turned onto a well-trod path, which narrowed as they progressed. Conversation ended when they were forced into single file. The spoken word was replaced by unspoken awe as the woods thickened and beauty enveloped them. Tall, massive trunks reached to the sky like spires of a magnificent cathedral. Oaks and sycamores held their leafed branches upwards in a posture of prayer, while birds twittered and flew among them; squirrels chattered and scampered through them, raising their own form of praising hymn.

Even Lady Brienne forgot her concerns, a smile coming to her lips for the first time in months.

Glancing at her, Lady Phillippa saw it and gave a few small skips in celebration.

Suddenly two shots rang out, and everyone froze. Josh fumbled for the blunderbuss he had tied to the team's harness.

"Leave be," the baroness ordered quietly. "They were not near us. Whose land are we on?" she asked Miss Durham.

"Lord Pergrine's . . . and he allows no hunting other than for his own enjoyment. 'Tis likely a poor cottager seeking meat for his family's table."

"A poacher?" Josh asked contemptuously.

"You would be too," Sarita turned on him angrily,

18

"if you were charged high rents and given no improvements. Would you let your family slowly starve while his lordship's woods abound with game?"

"I meant nothing," the large lad said, retreating from her wrath.

"Calm yourself, child," Lady Phillippa said softly. "We wish no one to go hungry. Come, we tarry too long. Why, it must be past time for tea."

Sarita stamped forward, her anger still apparent. The three sisters exchanged understanding glances before following, realizing that Miss Durham's ire was directed against the selfish lord.

"Is that the rectory?" Lady Brienne called to Miss Durham a short time later as she spied a long, low roof ahead.

"No, but we do not have much farther to go." The young woman halted, a frown creasing her brow. "How thoughtless of me not to let you rest. I am sorry. At times I get so angry with . . . with the way matters lie that I forget all else. Father insists that patience is its own reward and that we should all practice it. He says time alone will change Lord Pergrine, but I would rather I were a man and could give his lordship a sound enough thrashing to change his ways now," she said heatedly.

"Bravo," cried Lady Imogene, clapping her hands.

Miss Durham's colour, heightened by anger, deepened even more.

"I did not mean to embarrass you, child," the countess assured her sincerely. "I have often felt the same way."

"We all agree with you, Miss Durham," the

baroness added, allowing a little warmth into her tone. "Unjust landlords deserve no less."

Recalling Josh's judgment of his "fair, just, and generous" mistresses, Sarita gave them a weak smile.

To end the young woman's discomfort, Lady Phillippa asked, "Is yon building a home? 'Tis an odd sort of building."

"It is what is left of Lord Pergrine's ancestral home, now in ruin," Sarita explained.

"But smoke rises from one of the chimneys. Does someone live there?" Lady Imogene asked.

"Monsieur Mandel and his son, Pierre, live there. They came here after the terror in France and, strangely, Lord Pergrine has allowed them to stay . . . without rent, rumour has it. M. Mandel experiments with plants—grains and flowers. His work is most interesting."

"His son is young?" Lady Phillippa inquired, her matchmaking senses alert.

"Pierre is near my age, slightly older perhaps, about three and twenty." Miss Durham wrinkled her nose at this uncommon interest. "Let us go now," she told them and strode forward before further questions could be broached.

The sun was casting long afternoon shadows, and the ladies had to shield their eyes as they emerged from the forest into a broad clearing.

"Lud," exclaimed Josh, his eyes widening at the sight of a huge daub and wattle manor house with two towers jutting from the southern face. It stood to one side of the clearing not far from them, unlike any rectory anyone in the group had ever seen. "That can't be a rectory," the footman stated.

"I did say it was singular," Miss Durham laughed. "We didn't know what to think of it when we first saw it either. It is even more impressive, almost imposing, from the carriage road."

"But where is the church?" Lady Imogene asked.

"It is quite hidden by the rectory. Come, I will show it to you after you have refreshed yourselves. The church is interesting in its own right, being older than the house and constructed entirely of wood. I find its porch intriguing and often sit beneath its roof during the cool of the evening just to think. The church dates from the sixteenth century, with the rectory built before the close of the century," she added as they walked towards the manor house.

"But how did so vast a rectory come to be built here?" Lady Brienne questioned.

"It was not built as a rectory, but as the home of a man called Malvern. Legend has it that he did some terrible deed which haunted him, and he wished to be near a church, even though he had a chapel built within the house.

"The tale also tells that prayer and proximity to the church proved unhelpful to the poor man. He hung himself in the Hall one night. But he had deeded the house to the Church before doing so, and when the original rectory was destroyed by fire shortly afterwards, it was decided that the manor would replace it.

"Father and Mother were rather startled when they first saw the manor," Miss Durham continued, "but we have grown accustomed to it. Of course we do not use all the rooms, only those necessary for our needs."

"Poor Mr. Malvern," Lady Phillippa sighed. "One may hope his giving the manor aided his soul's fate."

"There are those who claim his spirit still walks about in the Hall and nearby woods. When I was younger, I spent many a night in the Hall trying to remain awake so that I could see him. But alas, I always fell soundly asleep, and Mr. Malvern proved an exceptionally quiet spirit, for I never was awakened by him." Sarita laughed.

The others joined her, except for Lady Brienne who scowled in disapproval. "One should respect the departed," she noted primly.

"Oh, Brienne," the countess clucked. "Never mind her, Miss Durham. It was a delightful story."

Sobered by the baroness's comment, Sarita led them straight to the front of the manor house. "Let me show you to our sitting room," she said as she began walking up the steps to the massive entry doors which were recessed between the three-sided towers.

"Miss, what am I to do with the horses?" Josh asked, sensing he was about to be left standing on the carriage drive.

"Oh, the stable is to the east, just around the side of the rectory," she answered. "When you are finished, come to the kitchen at the back of the house," Sarita instructed with a smile.

"Thank you, miss. I'll fetch along the baskets then," the young footman said and led the team away.

"Now, your ladyships, I will take you to Mother. She must be finished with her class by now. Then I will see to tea for you." Using both hands, the small figure gave an expert twist to a metal knob on one of the doors, and it swung slowly open. "Fortunately the doors are managed by a system of weights," she explained, seeing the surprised looks on the three dowagers' faces. With a backward step she dipped into a light curtsy and motioned the ladies to enter.

Lady Imogene and Lady Phillippa swept forward, eager to see the interior of so unusual a minister's home. After a pause, Lady Brienne walked forward stiffly. She hesitated on the threshold at the sound of children's voices.

"Oh, dear," Sarita moaned. "You had best . . ." Her words were cut off by a mob of laughing, running children who flooded into the Hall and ran out through the door, bumping and turning the baroness about in their hasty departure. "Step aside," Miss Durham remarked lamely.

"So much for your assurances that the rectory is not overrun with children," Lady Brienne said scathingly as she righted her hat and tugged her skirt into place. "At least it cannot be said to be small." She straightened herself rigidly and marched in.

"But it was only Mother's class," Sarita began in protest, then shrugged and followed.

"My dear, what a magnificent example of a double hammerbeam ceiling," Lady Imogene exclaimed. "And the wall hangings . . . they are extraordinary! Phillippa, have you ever seen such fine work?" the countess continued as she peered at the tree-of-life design woven into the tapestry hanging above the ornate wood paneling on the lower half of the forty-foot wall.

"Sarita, is that . . ." A young woman entered the

Hall and stopped short at the sight of the three unknown women.

"We have guests, Deborah. Would you please tell Mother?" Sarita asked, edging to the fore.

"Has your sister come?" a soft voice called from behind Deborah.

"Yes, Mother," she answered. "Sarita, you can't mean it," Deborah hissed, joining her sister. "What will we do?" An indignant look was thrown at the dowagers, who stood grouped in the center of the hall.

"We shall return to our coach, Miss Durham," the baroness said disdainfully, overhearing the words.

"Whom do I hear, Deborah? I thought you said Sarita had returned?" A plump, delicate duplicate of Sarita walked daintily into the Hall. "Guests. We have guests? Oh, my." She began to wring her hands, distress clouding her features.

"It is all right, Mother." Sarita hurried to her side and put an arm about her. "My ladies, this is my mother, Esther Durham. Mother, I would like you to meet Lady Phillippa." She guided her to the spritely white-haired marchioness.

"You have a beautiful daughter, Mrs. Durham," Lady Phillippa smiled.

"This is Lady Imogene," Sarita continued, going to the ample-figured countess, hoping that her mother's silence would not be misconstrued.

"The rectory is so unusual, Mrs. Durham. The hall is magnificent," Lady Imogene assured her hesitant hostess.

"And Lady Brienne," the young woman ended.

"The Dowager Baroness Mickle," her ladyship added haughtily, ending with a gasp.

Only Sarita saw the hasty kick dealt Lady Brienne's shin by Lady Phillippa.

"Mother, I am certain our guests would enjoy the sitting room. Their coach has been disabled, and their coachman has gone to Pordean to seek aid with the repairs."

"But wouldn't the solarium be more . . . Oh, yes, my class . . ."

"Are you truly a baroness?" Deborah stepped nearer as she interrupted her mother.

"Oh, Deborah, would you put water on for tea?" Sarita maneuvered towards the Hall's exit nearest the kitchen.

"Are they really titled? All three of them?" her sister whispered excitedly.

"Yes, and be quick about the tea.

"My ladies," Sarita turned back to them. "Follow me, please. Mother." She took her hand and led the way. After seeing that everyone was seated, Miss Durham excused herself and dashed for the kitchen at the far end of the house.

"You left Mother alone with them?" Deborah paled at the sight of her sister.

"You know she does quite well just visiting."

A pounding at the kitchen's outer door swung her around. "It is only young Mr. Caine, the ladies' footman," Sarita assured Deborah, hurrying to open the door. "Let me help you," she told Josh, reaching for one of the baskets he carried.

"Watch it ain't too heavy for you. Lud, you're a strong one for all your lack of size," he added admiringly. Setting the other basket down, he snatched his hat from his head and bobbed a bow at Deborah.

"This is my sister, Miss Deborah Durham."

"Pleased, miss." He bowed once more and shifted his weight uneasily.

"Did you find all you needed for the horses' comfort?" Sarita asked.

"Yes, miss. And I'll fetch the other basket right away." Josh bobbed another awkward bow and fled.

"What a clumsy lad," Deborah laughed.

"That is unkind," Sarita admonished. "Let us see what is inside these." She removed the towel covering the basket's contents and gave a sigh of relief. "This *has* to be a tin of tea."

"I wondered at your promising them tea."

"Our herbal tea is not distasteful," Sarita defended. "But let us hurry."

"Yes, you still have to do something about supper, and what are you going to do about this eve? Their coach will never be repaired in time to carry them on. Are they truly of the peerage? Their traveling gowns seem rather old."

"I know only that they are elderly widows and our guests. And it is their tea we are now serving. Do hurry along with it while I run to the garden. Father will be returning soon also." Just outside the kitchen door Sarita encountered Josh. "Set the basket on the table with the others and take an apple or two. You must be famished. I'll call you as soon as supper is ready," Sarita told him hurriedly and ran towards the vegetable garden. The largest of the tender young carrots were quickly pulled, and she was pinching off spinach greens when a shadow loomed before her.

26

"Best o' the day, Miss Sarita." A burly young man stood before her. "Thought you . . . that is, thought that Reverend Durham and all might enjoy these." He held forth three large hares.

"You are God sent, Clem," she said, almost hugging him in her relief. "Now supper will be complete. Nay," she laughed, "possible."

"Well, ah, thank you, Miss Sarita. I can dress 'em if you wish." he stammered, turned awkward by her evident pleasure.

"Do and you'll have some rabbit pie come tomorrow. You truly save me, Clem, for we have guests."

"That young lad I saw be one of them?" he asked. "Wondered. I best be at my task." He pulled his knife from a side sheath.

"Bring them to the kitchen when you're done," Sarita told the thick-set young farmer, gathering the carrots and spinach leaves in her skirt. Yanking some leeks from the ground as she passed them, she ran back to the kitchen.

"The tea is excellent, very similar to our own blend," Lady Imogene complimented Deborah as Mrs. Durham refilled her cup.

"Are you certain there are no biscuits?" Mrs. Durham asked her daughter for a third time.

Her cheeks tinged red from the countess's words, Deborah shook her head. "You were speaking of your journey?" She encouraged Lady Imogene to take up the conversation, hoping to divert her mother's attention from the lack of biscuits.

"So fortunate you are . . . to be able to travel at will," Mrs. Durham said just as the countess began to speak. "I did so before my marriage to Reverend Durham. Perhaps you are acquainted with my brother, Mr. Incole? We are second cousins to Baron Snold of Bath." She smiled hopefully.

"I fear we know neither gentleman," Lady Phillippa replied softly.

"But where is your baggage?" Mrs. Durham's mind changed direction.

"There is no need to be concerned. We shall return to our coach as soon as we finish our tea," Lady Brienne announced.

"Oh, but you mustn't," Mrs. Durham protested. "You must remain with us. How silly of me not to think of it before. How delightful to have guests." She clapped her hands, her mood altered once more. "Deborah, see to the guest rooms. Those nearest your room, I believe, will suit best. Remove the dust covers and ready them. This shall be grand," she rattled on excitedly.

"Confound it, where is everyone?" a deep voice sounded through the open sitting room door. "Sarita! Deborah?"

"Oh, dear, your father has been upset by something." Mrs. Durham rose agitatedly. She hurried to the door and called, "We are here, in the sitting room."

"Do you know what Lord Pergrine has done now?" the voice thundered nearer. "I may have to use Sarita's methods yet and horsewhip some sense into that confounded man." The words preceeded the medium-built, dark-haired rector into the room.

"Oh, Father," Deborah groaned while Mrs. Durham quailed.

The three dowagers gave each other faint smiles. Even Lady Brienne forgot herself momentarily and smiled as she thought how interesting this was becoming.

Chapter III

"Why are you in the sitting room this time of day?" Reverend Durham asked as he entered. Seeing the three older women, he apologized with a gracious bow. "My pardon, I had no idea we had guests."

"Never fear," Lady Phillippa smiled. "It is comforting to know that the ministers of the Lord are plagued just as we." She winked mischievously.

Reverend Durham looked questioningly over his wife's head to Deborah for some explanation of the present invasion.

"Father, this is Lady Phillippa, Lady Imogene, and Lady Brienne." She motioned to each. "Their coach has suffered a mishap, and they shall be spending the eve with us." Deborah ended uncertainly.

"Were you on your way to visit Lord Pergrine?" Reverend Durham asked abruptly.

"We are unacquainted with his lordship, but his welcome might prove more Christian," the baroness returned, her voice cold and hard.

Contriteness at once washed over the firmly built face. "My humble apologies once more, my ladies. I did not mean to be brusque. The times here have bred a disagreeable caution. You are most welcome in our home, but I feel honour bound to add that your staying with us will probably not increase your welcome at Lord Pergrine's."

"The little we have heard of his lordship does not incline us to value his opinion. Am I not correct, sisters?" Lady Brienne asked.

Both nodded in agreement.

A weary smile came to the minister's face. "Would my eldest, Sarita, have anything to do with your estimation?"

"We found your daughter most pleasant, and I daresay truthful in most matters," the baroness noted.

"I did not mean to imply the contrary," Reverend Durham returned with a wry smile, straightening from his tired, slumped stance. "She is merely opinionated and rightfully so, I fear."

"John, you are exhausted." Mrs. Durham fluttered to his side. "Please sit and have a cup of tea. Sarita is . . . seeing to supper, I suppose," she ended, frowning quizzically.

"Yes, Reverend Durham, don't stand on our account. We place little value on formality," Lady Phillippa urged him while motioning to a chair near her own.

"Has your fatigue to do with Lord Pergrine?" Lady Brienne questioned, giving him her full attention.

Sitting with welcome relief, Reverend Durham slowly sipped at the refreshing tea, then answered, "There have been long-standing problems in our area, but until late they were of tolerable proportions." Creases of concern hardened the lines about his eyes. "These past few years Lord Pergrine has raised his rents but has refused to make repairs or allow funds for new equipment and other necessary improvements. As a result, the bad will which already existed has fermented." Anger appeared in the calm, brown eyes. "Six months ago his lordship had an honest man, who was well-liked and respected, whipped and sent to gaol for poaching. Tempers exploded. Matters worsened when he had the man's wife and children removed from their cottage—a mere hovel. The men of the area swarmed like angry hornets to Pergrine Manor, but his lordship was ready for them with a crew of hired brigands. Luckily no one was killed in the fray. Since then there has been an incident each month. Lord Pergrine keeps his hold with the use of his ruffians. Three men have died . . . murdered for no known reason."

"Three? But there have only been two . . ." Deborah's voice trailed off as comprehension dawned. "Who?" she breathed.

"Old Taylor."

"But who would want to harm that kind old man?"

"I don't know. But the deed has been done. If you ladies will excuse me," Reverend Durham rose tiredly, "I must prepare something for the service on the morrow."

"You believe Lord Pergrine is involved in these deaths?" Lady Brienne asked speculatively.

Shaking his head, the minister answered, "I do not know, my lady, but something must be done." He rubbed his brow, then bowed. "I shall see you at supper."

"It was very thoughtful of Miss Durham to have Josh and that young Mr. Traunt fetch our portmanteaux from the coach," Lady Imogene noted as the three sisters gathered in Lady Brienne's chamber after having excused themselves for the evening.

They had been given a set of three interconnecting bedchambers on the west side of the rectory's upper storey, between Sarita and Deborah's shared chamber in the tower at the front and Reverend and Mrs. Durham's at the rear of the manor house.

"Did you notice how exhausted Miss Sarita looked at supper?" Lady Philippa asked, plopping down on the baroness's bed. "One would have thought she had readied our rooms and cooked supper, too."

"I thought it a trifle odd that there was no one to serve supper other than the daughters," said Lady Imogene, joining the marchioness on the bed, "but it was a most succulent stew. I have never tasted better. 'Twas odd, though. As delicious as the stew was, I could not quite decide on the meat. A distinctive flavour. What did you think of it, Brienne?"

The baroness turned from the dressing table's looking glass to face the bed. "It was . . . edible."

" 'Pon my soul, my lady, is that why you had third portions," teased Lady Phillippa with a gentle laugh. "It was good to see you with such a hearty appetite, Brenny," she said, becoming quite serious.

"I was uncommonly hungry. The walk, I imagine. But come, let us turn our minds to more serious matters than supper's fare. Have there not been many suspicious . . . nay, mysterious occurrences hinted at?"

"Oh, Brienne, are we going to stay?" Lady Imogene clapped her plump hands in delighted anticipation. "I had so hoped we would. The architectural features of this house are amazing. I could add so much to my notes on sixteenth-century manor houses."

"Yes, and we have those two lovely young women,"

Lady Phillippa took up the conversation, "although I must admit to being partial to Miss Sarita. Do you think she favours Mr. Traunt? Did she not call him Clem?"

"My ladies, I was not thinking of such nonsense," Lady Brienne interrupted their ramblings. "No. I was wondering about the Durhams' odd behaviour and this Lord Pergrine. He presents a complicated shadow. Even allowing for the eccentricities of an autocratic lord, he has handled matters strangely. I would like to meet the man."

"If your mind insists on such a turn," said Lady Imogene, "why not ponder why he allows two Frenchmen to reside there for no apparent rent, while plaguing his lifelong tenants."

"Exactly." Lady Brienne pounced on the words, her eyes bright and full of life. "There is much to be learned here."

"But how will we manage it?" Lady Phillippa questioned eagerly. "Oh, Brenny, you have a plan!"

"Perhaps." She leaned back contemplatively. "Let us sleep well, and on the morrow we shall see what Mr. Caine has learned. It would not surprise me if the wheelwright in Pordean has proven unhelpful. Don't you recall Sarita's reaction?"

Lady Imogene, who had not been paying attention, wondered aloud, "Mrs. Durham is an odd one for a minister's wife. Do you sense that somehow she is being shielded by the family? One moment she appears the same as you and I, and yet . . ."

"There is a fragility of the mind," the marchioness agreed.

"Miss Durham—Sarita, that is—certainly has none,"

the baroness gave an assessing compliment, "despite the daintiness of her slender form. She strikes me as quite sensible and very capable, no matter what the task given her."

At this moment the capable Miss Durham was trudging slowly towards the stairs, her shoulders slumped, her dark hair frizzed from standing over hot dishwater.

"Sarita, how are you, child?" Reverend Durham came from the shadows. "Didn't Deborah . . . ?"

"I sent her to bed a short time ago. She was exhausted."

"And you?"

"A day's work, well done, is not harmful." She attempted to smile.

"If the dowagers are to remain another day, I insist you get Tessy to help. Now don't object. Her husband has been wanting someone to repair his longcase clock, and you know she misses helping out here."

"But you haven't time enough now for all you do," Sarita objected.

"Who just said a day's work, well done, does no harm?" He laughed, putting his arm about her shoulders.

"A day's work, not a night's too," she returned sharply.

"We are both tired and morn shall come before we would have it." Reverend Durham kissed his daughter's brow. "Well done, little princess . . . we named you well." Pride glowed in his eyes as he looked at her tenderly.

Sarita raised on tiptoe and brushed her father's

cheek with a kiss. "The 'little' I cannot deny," she shook her head, "but my day's tasks are not those of a princess. But . . . Good sleep, Father." She trudged up the stairs.

The hushed whispers coming from Lady Brienne's bedchamber caught Sarita's attention as she neared the door; she had imagined the three would be quickly asleep after the day's excitement. A sudden bubble of laughter floating from the room halted her. Drawn by curiosity, she slowly edged closer to the door.

"Yes," she overheard the baroness, "I imagine Mr. Caine will be truly relieved when he finds our note. I think the dear man thought us finally gone mad after our last halt. But here we have acceptable rooms . . ."

"Don't forget the edible food," mimicked Lady Imogene.

"A welcome respite from . . ." Lady Phillippa began.

Sarita forced herself to walk on. It was as she had thought. These ladies, titled or not, two sweet and one slightly sour, were upon hard times. *Why, I wonder . . . does the coach really need repair?* she asked herself, stepping quietly into her shared bedchamber. Ah, well, pride is a hard taskmaster. Her thoughts continued as she undressed and washed herself. Sarita then pulled on her nightdress, extinguished the candle, and sat upon the bed.

Savouring the softness of the feather bed, she eased between the cool sheets and slowly relaxed.

"Sarita, are you still awake?" Deborah's whispered question reached her from across the room.

"No," she answered.

"What do you think of the ladies?" Eagerness echoed in her words.

"At this moment I would like to not think of them," Sarita threw back softly, thinking of all the tasks that lay before her on the morrow because of the trio.

"I think they have been sent to us," Deborah said with firm conviction. "You know how I have been praying we would be released from this place."

"And how are their ladyships going to assist us in that?" Sarita's aching body resisted her compassionate nature. "Are you thinking of becoming their abigail?"

"You know Father would never permit such a thing! Indeed, why should I become an abigail?" her sister challenged indignantly.

"We are both tired, Debs. To sleep." Sarita turned over and hugged her pillow, her eyes refusing to remain open any longer.

"Oh, Sarita, listen to me. Isn't it possible they shall be grateful for all our care and attention while their coach is being repaired? They seem favourably impressed by Father, and Mother has told them of our connection with Lord Snold."

"What has that to do with anything?" Sarita mumbled.

"Why, don't you see? They will return to London and send for us. I just know it," Deborah whispered excitedly. "Imagine what it would be like to be among real lords and ladies, especially the eligibles. Think; we could make splendid matches, perhaps even gain a title."

Sarita heard the words as she slowly drifted into a deep sleep. "Lords and ladies," she mouthed and a wry laugh escaped as dreams of richly dressed dancers swirled into her mind to the tempo of the forbidden waltz. The dowagers edged into the vision clothed in rich brocades. Strands of pearls and jewels weighted their necks. Deborah stood beside them, similarly bedecked. Then Sarita saw herself, in plain dove brown, scurrying too and fro trying to satisfy all.

Suddenly Pierre Mandel and Clem Traunt appeared, both urging her to come. Just as she was about to step forward a hand stayed her, and she turned and saw her mother.

Awakening with a start, Sarita shook the feeling of dread away as she realized it was her mother's voice she heard calling. Her feet touched the floor before she even thought to go.

Lady Brienne also heard Mrs. Durham's fearful calls and rose. She eased her door open after she heard Sarita's footsteps hurry past and followed. Listening to the soft crooning of the young woman's voice, the baroness heard a heavy tread on the stairs and hastened to hide in another doorway.

"I'll care for her now," she heard Reverend Durham speak. "You need your rest. She is calmer now; it will pass. Go on."

Waiting until Sarita had returned to her room, Lady Brienne scurried down the hall to her own bedchamber. There was much to be learned on the morrow.

Chapter IV

Wild whoops of childish mischievousness and scurrying feet echoed into the vast Hall, where Lady Imogene was studying the intricacies of the wood carving above the huge fireplace on the north wall. Mrs. Durham's plaintive voice rose and fell amid the uproar. The countess's usual absorption was broken repeatedly by these distractions, and she finally laid aside her note pad and began an angry waddle towards the door.

"Why Imogene, what has bristled your ire?" Lady Brienne questioned as she entered the Hall, surprised to see her usually placid sister moving at such a fast pace, and even more confounded by the uncommon scowl upon her round face. "Where is that tumult coming from?" she asked, a fresh burst of cacophonous sound echoing into the Hall. "Surely not from Mrs. Durham's class?"

Lady Imogene's head bobbed assent. "It has been like this ever since the children arrived," she snorted.

The bedlam peaked and then diminished. A door slammed. Mrs. Durham stalked past one of the Hall's entrances.

"It appears the barbarians have been victorious," the baroness noted dryly. "Let us review the horde."

"But they are . . . children," Lady Imogene gasped. "You . . . well, you dislike children, Brienne. Besides, what can we possibly do with them?" she questioned.

"I know you often taught your own two children, Imogene. Don't deny it. Follow me."

Utter silence fell as the two elderly women entered the solarium. They surveyed the suddenly frozen panorama of mischief.

"Boys, replace the inkwells and release the girls," Lady Brienne ordered curtly. "You smaller children, pick up your slates and papers from the floor." As the children scurried about, the two dowagers walked to the raised dais at one end of the room.

One of the larger boys decided to challenge these new adversaries. "We ain't got to do what you says. Mrs. Durham be teacher here, and she says class be o'er fer the day."

The other children paused, awaiting the outcome.

"Your name, young man?" the baroness asked softly.

"Lum. Lum Wicket. And I says we're leavin'."

"Mr. Wicket, would you care to be pilloried? I happened to see such a device, placed nearby most conveniently, during my walk this morn."

"Ha! Ye wouldn't . . . couldn't put me in it." He laughed derisively.

"I am the Dowager Baroness of Mickle, and this," she motioned to Lady Imogene, "is the Dowager Countess of Lackland. Now, will you assist the others, or do I call my footmen who are waiting just beyond the door?" she asked with iron-toned coldness, her eyes hard upon the lad.

The boy wavered, the manner of this lady being far afield from Mrs. Durham. His eyes fell from her gaze, and he bent to retrieve a slate board at his feet. Following his example, the others returned to their work. Soon the solarium was restored to order, the unruly students quietly seated awaiting the Baroness Mickle's pleasure.

Looking at each child individually, Lady Brienne spoke. "You are here for the rudiments of an education and so shall it be. We," she motioned to herself and her sister, "shall conduct today's class."

The gasp coming from Lady Imogene was matched by one in the baroness's own mind. *You cannot tolerate children, much less instruct them. Have you gone mad?* she asked herself. "Take up your slates and let us see what you have learned thus far," her voice continued despite an inner quailing.

The warm June day had brought small beads of perspiration to Sarita's forehead as she plucked weeds from among the spinach plants. Straightening and stretching to ease her aching back, she saw her mother ambling along the edge of the woods which ran behind the garden and rectory. "Mother, have you dismissed your class early?" she called out, raising her skirts and stepping haphazardly over the rows of vegetables.

"Class? Did I have class today?" Mrs. Durham asked. "Oh, yes, I believe I did, but that was much earlier," she said with a happy smile, dispelling the confusion which had raised Sarita's suspicions. "I am going for a walk, my dear."

"Mother, your class? Did Deborah help you with it?" Sarita asked as she reached her mother's side.

"I sent her to the Swaites with some of those lovely

41

apples the ladies gave us. You know the grandmother has been feeling poorly."

"But the children, did they leave?"

Mrs. Durham reached out and patted Sarita's hand. "You fret far too much, my dear. Why don't you walk with me?" She smiled brightly.

"No, Mother, you go on. I will finish the weeding," Sarita told her.

"Such a good daughter," the older woman sighed. "You work far too much. I must speak with your father . . ." Without completing the thought, she sauntered off.

Sarita watched her mother's back for a few moments, then picked up her skirts and dashed past the church to the kitchen door. Halting to regain her breath, she leaned against the kitchen table, gasping for air. It is quiet, she thought, too much so. Half-running, she made her way towards the solarium. Apprehension slowed her steps as she neared the chamber.

The measured tones of recitation caused Sarita to pause outside the door. Had Deborah returned in time to take the class? She shook her head. No, even Debs had difficulty controlling the youngsters. Slowly she eased the door open and was utterly astonished to see Lady Imogene working quietly with the youngest children in one corner and Lady Brienne solemnly listening to the older ones reciting verses from the Bible.

Seeing Sarita, the baroness nodded imperiously to her while saying, "Very good, Mr. Wicket. That will be all for today. Class will be held before services on Sunday for the remainder of the summer season. Be prompt. You may go as soon as Countess Lackland finishes."

Lady Imogene bade her students return to their benches after a few moments and joined the baroness on the dais.

In one body the children rose. The boys bowed while the girls curtsied. They all straightened awkwardly. "Good day, Baroness Mickle, Countess Lackland," came as a general murmur. Then slowly, silently, they filed past Sarita out of the solarium.

"Close your mouth, child," the baroness said with a slow smile.

"What did you do to them?" Sarita managed to say.

"They did do rather well for us, didn't they?" the baroness smiled widely. "But tell me, how has your father persuaded the people to allow them to come?"

"And how did you know this was to be the last week of class?" Awe, suspicion were mixed in Sarita's tones and look.

"This season is far too busy for the farmers to permit their children to come to class when they can be working in the fields. Since this week began in May, I concluded it had to be the last for classes."

"Well, thank you for . . . for helping Mother. She does well unless distressed, then she withdraws . . . recalls only what she wishes . . ."

"Never mind, my dear," Lady Imogene came to Sarita's rescue. "We enjoyed it. Perhaps we could conduct the Sunday classes for as long as we remain?"

"But surely your coach will be repaired in a few days," the young woman exclaimed, then blushed at the force of her words.

"Sadly not. It appears there will be an indefinite

delay. Mr. Caine told us earlier this morn that the wheelwright in Pordean has a very large order from Lord Pergrine and will not be able to make a new axle for our coach for well nigh a month. As there is no wheelwright in Runnet, we have decided . . ."

"Could you not send Mr. Caine to Hastings to fetch an axle?" Sarita asked hopefully.

"Impossible," Lady Brienne said adamantly. "We have instructed Mr. Caine to solicit help in removing the coach from its present position and bring it here. I believe your Mr. Traunt is aiding them."

"He is not my Mr. Traunt," Sarita shot back defensively. "You will be here for some time then." She blanched slightly.

"If your father consents to our staying," the baroness said gently, wondering why the young woman was so dismayed.

"Oh," Sarita shrugged hopelessly but tried to smile. "I am certain he shall." She went back towards the door. Reaching it, she halted. "Thank you . . . for your help with the class."

"You never did say how your father convinced the farmers," Lady Imogene noted curiously.

Blushing furiously, Sarita stammered. "It is . . . it is because Mother holds the classes, and Lord Pergrine is aware that everyone knows of her weakness . . ." Tears welled in her eyes. "I must go. If you care to take the classes, it will be appreciated. I . . . I must return to the weeding," she choked out and ran down the corridor.

"The poor child was about to cry. Now why?" Lady Imogene questioned aloud.

"Lord Pergrine becomes less likeable and more of a

puzzle at each turn. Let us find Phillippa. I had the most unusual experience during my walk. Do you recall mention of the Frenchmen?" Lady Brienne spoke as they left the solarium, making their way towards the front doors.

"Where do you think Phillippa could be?" Lady Imogene asked as the two halted on the front steps of the rectory. "The stables, perhaps?"

"No, our teams are with Mr. Caine, and Josh said Reverend Durham has only one poor beast, which he took this morn."

"Isn't it odd for a rector to have only one horse?"

"There are many strange things about the rector, his family, and his people."

The two had gone down the steps and ambled towards the east as they spoke with one another. On this side of the rectory the remnants of a once-grand garden struggled to maintain shreds of its past glory. Lady Phillippa, wandering through it, saw her sisters.

"Brenny, Immy, here in the garden." She fluttered a wave. "Join me." When the two neared her, she smiled conspiratorily. "I have been thinking and have decided that Sarita . . ."

"First let me tell you what happened during my walk," the baroness interrupted. "Let us go to the arbour at the back there," she pointed. "No one will overhear us."

"What should no one overhear?" Lady Imogene questioned tartly as she and the marchioness exchanged knowing shrugs. When Brienne's voice took on this tone, there was no halting her.

After casting about to see if anyone was near, Lady Brienne sat beside her sisters. In a hushed whisper she told of having followed the path which Sarita had led them over. "I spied a man walking ahead of me and hastened my steps, but suddenly he was gone. My first thought was that he was a poacher, but he carried no hunting piece or game. I spied a suspicious splash of white and crept forward. It was another man. I could not see them clearly, for I feared going closer, but I did overhear their conversation, in French. How fortunate it was I and not you who chanced upon them," she said in an aside to Lady Phillippa, arching her brow. "The one in white was called Pierre, mayhap the Pierre Mandel Sarita spoke of. They talked of an arrival and the need to arrange cover and that transportation should be ready."

"What could that mean?" Lady Imogene puzzled.

"Probably just that they are smuggling in some French brandy." Lady Phillippa dismissed Brienne's intimation of worse.

"But what if it isn't something so harmless as brandy?" asked Lady Brienne. "Why does young Mandel need to meet with anyone secretly? His father surely would not disapprove of such smuggling? No, I feel it is far more serious than spirits."

"Countess? Lady Phillippa? Baroness Mickle?" the three heard Sarita's voice calling them.

Rising at once, they stepped forward. The baroness's eyes narrowed at the sight of the white-shirted young man at Sarita's side.

"You were correct, Mademoiselle Durham. The *mesdames sont très belles.*" He bowed with a flourish, the ruffles on his cuffs fluttering softly.

"Monsieur Mandel, this is Lady Imogene, Countess of Lackland; Lady Phillippa, Marchioness of Bawden, and Lady Brienne, Dowager Baroness of Mickle. My ladies, Monsieur Pierre Mandel."

"*C'est mon plaisir, mesdames.*"

"*Merci.* Do you not find life here strange, Monsieur Mandel . . . after having lived in France all your life?" Lady Brienne asked lightly.

"With friends such as you English, how can life be but pleasing?" He shrugged languidly. "Especially with the companionship of one such as Mademoiselle Sarita." Mandel put an arm passionately about the young woman's shoulders.

Frowning at this intimacy, Sarita edged away from him.

The glint of disapproval in his eye as she did so was noted by Lady Brienne. "A young man as handsome as yourself must be kept *très occupé*," she said.

The arrogance of the man flashed briefly as he preened in response to the compliment. Brushing a speck of dust from the ruffles of his shirt-front, his eyes stole to Sarita, then snapped back to the baroness. "You speak *français, madame*?"

"Only a few phrases. My late husband was fond of the language." Lady Brienne smiled.

"Perhaps you could tell us of your home, Monsieur Mandel?" Lady Phillippa spoke with interest. "We travelled extensively in France many years ago."

"Then you speak our language?" he questioned, his eyes narrowing.

"A kind not understood by Frenchmen," Lady Brienne said, startling Sarita with a trilling laugh. "We found we could comprehend each other but not the French nor they us," she twittered.

Pierre smiled, relief showing in his eyes. "During

my morning walk I thought I saw one of you. You, Madame Mickle, *n'etait-ce pas?*"

"Only if you were on the path in the woods leading to the road where our coach is mired," she tossed back lightly. "I started out for our coach, but an unusual bird lured me from the path. "Unfortunately," her face saddened, "I was unable to locate the bird."

"I wish you better fortune next time," he bowed. "Now I must take leave of you. It is my hope we shall meet again during your stay," Mandel said oilily. Turning to Sarita, he took her hand and kissed it.

Till next we meet, *m'amie,*" he said lowly, then sauntered away.

Three pairs of eyes followed his swaggering steps, then turned to a red-faced Sarita.

"I must attend to my duties," she said, angry at Mandel's presumptuous behaviour. "Supper will be served at the same time as last eve." She stalked away.

"Methinks the young lady dislikes yon Frenchman," Lady Brienne noted dryly.

"She is not alone in that feeling," Lady Phillippa murmured.

"What was it you decided about Sarita?" Lady Imogene questioned the marchioness, recalling her earlier comment.

"First let me tell you about a conversation I had with a Mrs. Tessy O'Neal," Lady Phillippa said, motioning them back into the arbour. "Mrs. O'Neal would do for a dragoon in the King's army." She winked as she sat down. "It appears she has a partiality for the Durhams and resents our imposition here."

"Imposition," blustered the baroness.

"Hear me out, Brenny." Lady Phillippa smiled at

her sister's reaction. "I feel you could take a strong liking to Mrs. O'Neal, pardon me, to Tessy. I am under command to use her given name only. She has your 'tactful' approach, Brienne." With a mischievous wink at Lady Imogene she continued, "Which explains why I rather felt like I was being trampled the first few moments of our talk. I must say it was a rather unique feeling, being identified with light skirts at my age. Well, what was I to think," the marchioness explained with a shrug and a laugh, "when Tessy greeted me with, 'Are you one of *those* women?'"

The baroness clucked, but Lady Imogene burst into laughter.

Feigning seriousness, Lady Phillippa continued, "When you see Tessy's proportions, you will know how far she outranks my title." She nodded at Lady Brienne's grimace. "She has in the past been nursemaid, cook . . . of general service to the Durhams. In fact, she did so until two years past when, according to Tessy, Lord Pergrine began seriously dissuading his tenants from attending the Church or supporting it."

"But why?" said the countess.

The baroness bristled.

"Reverend Durham had begun speaking out against Pergrine's high rents and other injustices to his tenants," Lady Phillippa explained.

"How have the Durhams gone on without support? Is he of independent means?" Lady Brienne asked.

The marchioness shook her head. "Not from what I have learned. They are nearly pauperized, from what Tessy has told me. Only a few now dare to contribute to the Church. Some people give them food, but furtively, to escape Pergrine's retribution," she ended.

"But if the Durhams have no servants and little food, who has been doing all the cooking, cleaning, washing?" Lady Imogene wondered aloud. "Where has the food come from these past three days?"

"It could only be Sarita," the baroness responded. "She has looked increasingly worn. Something must be done." She stood up abruptly. "Let us send Mr. Caine for our Meg and her girls."

"No."

The baroness and the countess were surprised at Lady Phillippa's vehemence.

"The Durhams would refuse any help given in that way," Lady Phillippa said. "They are proud. Besides, I suspect they think we have seen better times and I do not wish to dispel that idea as yet."

"Then what would you suggest?" Lady Brienne demanded. "We cannot let the child continue to do everything."

"Exactly," Lady Phillippa concurred. "Since we are the cause of the extra labour, why don't we provide the help?"

"Help? Personally?" Lady Imogene echoed weakly.

"Yes, Immy. You were a tolerable cook at one time . . ."

"Tolerable!" The pudgy countess straightened. "Only the best cook in the shire," she blustered. "But that was many years past," she said uncertainly.

"And what, may I ask, have you planned for me?" Lady Brienne challenged.

"Why, our home at Hawkhurst was always the

neatest. And of course, you would only be supervising Sarita and Deborah," she ended hopefully.

"And you?" both sisters asked the marchioness in unison.

"Tessy has agreed to handle the laundry. There is the mending and many small tasks I can see to. Oh, come, you two, we will enjoy it. It is only for a short time. Are we not agreed to it?" Her eyes flew eagerly from one to the other.

Chapter V

A soft breeze gently fanned Sarita as she sat beneath the huge old oak tree near the kitchen door. Its shade was refreshingly cool after the heat of the sun, which had shone full upon her in the garden moments before. Peas were pushed from their pods and fell into the pan in Sarita's lap with clattering vigour until the bottom was covered. Beside her the heap of emptied pods grew steadily, but glancing into her pan Sarita wondered if she would ever have enough for supper. Resisting the urge to throw the peas she had already shelled to the wind, she shook her head, a heavy sigh escaping. *Why don't I do like Deborah?* she thought. *Mother would not have objected to my going with them, and I enjoy the Dollard sisters. Think, they are about to have tea and . . .*

"Tea! Oh, dear, I forgot tea," Sarita bemoaned, then stiffened her tone. "Tea will just have to be late," she pronounced, a defiant sentence on the afternoon repast.

"Of course it will not be late." Lady Imogene's voice startled her.

The young woman jumped up, nearly upsetting the shelled peas. "But I cannot prepare . . ." she began angrily, turning to confront the countess. Her words died, and her eyes grew large at the sight of the tea tray in the woman's hands.

"Carefully, carefully," Lady Phillippa admonished Sarita, taking the pan from her unsteady hands.

"But . . ."

"Do sit down, Miss Durham," the baroness commanded. "I do not care to take my tea standing."

"But you should not be serving," Sarita objected, still confused.

" 'Tis only a cup of tea," Lady Phillippa objected, placing the pan on the ground. Mr. Caine and Ben set down chairs, and the dowagers sat down.

Sarita continued dumbfounded as tea was served. "You act as if this were a regular occurrence," she managed at last.

"And why not?" Lady Imogene asked, smiling.

"But you are . . . ladies. Titled."

"Titled by marriage only," Lady Brienne returned.

"We were once simple daughters of a mere fourth son," Lady Phillippa explained, "whose marriages brought love, not fortunes. Our lives then and now are much as yours."

Sarita was unconvinced. "I . . . I really do not have time for tea," she began to excuse herself.

"Tsk, tsk. So impatient," Lady Imogene reproved. "Rushing is bad for the complexion."

But not for your supper, Sarita wished to say aloud.

"Phillippa and I will manage this eve's meal. You are to rest," the countess assured the surprised young woman.

"Yes," Lady Phillippa smiled. "I would not wish you to be worn looking when . . . Well, you do need your rest," she ended under her sisters' questioning glances.

53

"Do you not wish us to help or do you fear we are incompetent?" Lady Brienne asked a dubious Sarita.

"Why . . . why, neither. I just . . . Father will . . ."

"Will see the justice in it, never fear," Lady Imogene assured her. "Brienne will see to that. Now come along and show us the kitchen. We did manage tea, and after all these years I find the prospect of cooking rather tantalizing."

"Let us hope the results also are," the baroness noted dryly, then smiled.

Laughing, Lady Phillippa and Lady Imogene took Sarita by the hands and led her to the kitchen.

Reverend Durham, returning to the rectory later than usual, washed and hurried to the dining salon. Finding his wife anxiously pacing to and fro, he spoke her name softly. "Esther."

She whirled towards him, her face ashen.

"Esther, has something happened to Sarita . . . to Deborah?" he demanded, fearing the worst.

"No, no. They are both well," she answered in bewilderment.

"Then what has happened?" His voice softened.

"Good eve, Reverend Durham," Lady Brienne greeted the rector as she entered the room. "I see Sarita still has not risen." She nodded approvingly.

"Sarita is ill, then?" Reverend Durham questioned the baroness.

"She is as healthy as you and I. More so, I would think, with her few years," Lady Brienne told him. "Let us sit down; supper is about to be served."

Casting a dubious look at his wife, his questions still wanting answers, the minister moved to obey the authoritative tone. Seating his wife, he assisted Lady Brienne to her chair and then took his own.

"Good eve," Lady Phillippa greeted them all cheerfully as she hurried into the dining salon bearing a large, covered tray. Behind her Lady Imogene bustled along, carrying a steaming bowl of buttered fresh garden peas.

Reverend Durham leapt to his feet, consternation and indignation covering his features. "My ladies, I . . . Deborah, what is the reason for this?" he demanded of his daughter, who came in behind the countess with a tray of warm, newly baked bread. "Why are our guests serving us?" he demanded angrily.

"Reverend Durham." The baroness's icy voice made him turn to her. "If you will permit my sisters and Deborah to take their seats, we shall explain."

"Yes, my lady." A wry grin came to the minister's lips. "Pardon my . . . hasty ire."

"Most assuredly, Reverend," Lady Phillippa piped. "But you see, we simply could not remain idly by when we realized the situation."

"Situation?" he repeated hollowly.

"Lack of good help is always a problem in the country," the countess took up the explanation, "what with all the young girls seeking their fortunes in London. Three guests can prove a burden."

"Therefore we shall participate in the duties of the household till we depart," Lady Brienne said firmly to the amazed man. "Now, let us dine. I am famished."

Acceding since he saw no other choice, Reverend Durham led grace.

Tentative sampling began when he had ended and soon everyone concurred that Lady Imogene, beaming brightly as she watched them eagerly partaking, had not forgotten her culinary skills.

As appetites eased, conversation began flowing. "Reverend Durham," said Lady Brienne, "when you first entered the dining room tonight, you appeared very anxious upon not seeing Sarita. Did you actually fear that something had occurred to harm her?"

"Yes," he answered simply.

"Who would want to harm her?" Lady Phillippa gasped.

"She has no enemies . . . of her own," the minister assured them. Seeing his wife blanch, he laughed easily. "It was only the bothersome worry of a father. So many small things can occur in the most ordinary of days," he said, trying to dismiss the matter.

"Yes, so many things," the baroness agreed, with a smile at Mrs. Durham. Her eyes swept back to Reverend Durham, but he would not meet her gaze.

The dowagers, safely ensconced in Lady Brienne's chambers, had been animatedly discussing the day's happenings. They were speaking of Pierre Mandel when Lady Phillippa suddenly clapped her hands. "I just remembered my decision," she explained to her sisters, her eyes twinkling merrily.

"Ah, yes, Sarita," Lady Brienne nodded. "But if you intend to match her with Mandel, you are ready for Bedlam."

"What is this about a match for Sarita? Will you speak more plainly?" Lady Imogene demanded, pouting.

"You know 'decision' to Philly means 'match,' " the baroness frowned. "The poor girl had better beware."

"A match for Sarita? Excellent." The countess turned eagerly to Lady Phillippa. "But you cannot meant Mr. Traunt. A good man, to be sure, but . . ."

"Both of you are far from the mark," Lady Phillippa tossed back lanquidly.

"Perhaps the young woman does not wish to wed," Lady Brienne objected.

"That is what you yourself said until you met Baron Mickle," Lady Imogene poohed at her. "What better reward could there be for all the kindness Sarita has shown us than a good match?"

"Do you disapprove of a match, or of Sarita?" questioned the marchioness, wondering at the baroness's sudden sourness.

"Miss Durham is a fine young woman," said Lady Brienne irritably. "More sensible than most. I simply do not see why you must dabble in her affairs. She appears well enough content."

"Pay no mind to Brenny, Phillippa." Lady Imogene waved a pudgy hand dismissing her sister's objection. "Whom do you intend for her? Does Lord Pergrine have a marriageable son?"

"Poor choice that would be, even if one did exist," said the baroness coldly. "If you must pursue this, I pray you find someone worthy of the honour . . . and able to fend off whatever danger exists here."

"Oh, I think I have," smiled Lady Phillippa. "Would you say the Earl of Dunstan was a worthy enough individual?"

"Impossible!" scoffed Lady Brienne.

"How?" came from Lady Imogene. "We are far

from his usual ground. Besides, Henrietta would never permit it."

With a sparkling smile Lady Phillippa drew a letter from her pocket. "This afternoon I wrote this note," she began.

Chapter VI

"It should be clear to you, Lord Dunstan, that we must have someone near Hastings or at least near the coast in that area. Someone who can move about freely, unquestioned. Your rank would enable you to do this.

"These reports that Napoleon has managed to place someone in the area, who sends dispatches about our fortification efforts, have to be investigated. With all the preparations the First Consul is making for an invasion, we must take precautions. Why, we have had word that over one thousand transport craft are being built." The undersecretary paced to and fro under the calculating eyes of the Earl of Dunstan.

"If only we knew for certain who this man is," the undersecretary continued. "Lord Pergrine's estates are in the Hastings area and could be used as a base. Can you manage an invitation for an indefinite stay?"

"Lord Pergrine left London with the season only half accomplished," the earl drawled slowly.

The undersecretary waited patiently, his eyes lightly upon the brawny young man before him. Experience had taught him that the casual dress and oft indifferent ways of the earl were deceptive.

"Give me a day. I'll manage something." Dunstan flicked his gloves absently against the arm of his chair, then rose. His height was two inches under six feet, but his solid, firmly built form belied the fact. The broad, muscular shoulders were disguised by a loose-fitting coat, carelessly worn open. A simple cravat, unstarched in open defiance of the Beau's mandates, graced the thick neck. Form-fitting breeches showed smooth-muscled legs; dusty hessians completed his attire. "If there are questions on my report, send word to my house," he said. "I will remain in London for two or three days. Communiqués can be managed as usual when I reach the coast."

"Will you have ample time to set your personal affairs in order?" the undersecretary asked, also rising.

"You've never been concerned with that before," Dunstan smiled. "Perhaps you take my mother's gossip too seriously. I have no intention of wedding. Much to her dislike, Mother has become accustomed to my . . . meandering."

"You don't bloody well think she has guessed what you're about?" the startled man asked.

"No. Mother's thoughts have never taken a turn in that direction. Her machinations deal only with the serious problem of my lack of an heir." Dunstan said lightly, shrugging his wide shoulders. Seriously, he asked, "Have adequate preparations been made for a defense, should Napoleon prove intent upon this invasion?"

"We are safe enough until his transport craft are completed. After that . . ." The undersecretary's palms turned upwards in a gesture of hopelessness. "The local citizenry have been called to arms, but they are untrained and without reliable weapons or leaders . . . useless, in plain words. We desperately need the information you can get."

" 'Twill be yours. Now I must go. Wouldn't want to arouse suspicion by being too long."

The two men shook hands in farewell. Loosening his cravat and ruffling a hand through his already disarrayed curly dark brown hair, Dunstan sauntered from the private chamber at the Cat and Mouse Inn. With a broad smile and a wink at the innkeeper, he flipped the man a gold piece.

"Glad ta be a help, milord," the man smiled knowingly, returning the wink. "Is yer friend ta be usin' the back door?"

With a nod and a look that bespoke his reliance on the silence and trustworthiness of the innkeeper, Lord Dunstan ambled out into Covent Square. No one took note of him, for this establishment was known to be oft frequented by the *ton* in search of idle pleasure. The ragged boy holding the earl's bay stallion stared in wonder at the coin placed in his hand, enough to provide food for his family for a week.

Dunstan wended his mount skillfully through the crowded streets of London, halting only when he reached his bachelor quarters on Chesterfield Street.

"My lord, Mr. Sullivan awaits you in your study," the butler told him, taking the earl's hat and gloves.

"Have my phaeton with the matched blacks brought around in half an hour," Dunstan ordered, and strode briskly to his study. "Lindsay, good fellow, are the papers ready for my signature?" he greeted his cousin, who served as his agent and personal secretary.

The foppishly attired young man in a blue long coat, with white-and-blue striped lapels, narrow blue pantaloons, and black pumps, was three years younger than the earl's one and thirty years but his usual stern countenance, at odds with his mode of toilet, gave him the appearance of being ten years older.

His features lightened into a smile at sight of his cousin. "Cris, I was glad to learn you had returned once again." His brows arched in a rare glimpse of his humourous side. "How long will it be this time?" He held his hand out in greeting.

"Two . . . three days. Are there any letters of import among these?" The earl waved a hand at the stack of material awaiting his attention.

"There are the usual bids from those remaining in London and some rather heavily perfumed missives." Sullivan cocked his head pensively as they sat down, "and a note from your aunt, Lady Bawden."

"Aunt Philly? But I thought they were travelling. Where is it?" Dunstan looked up from the document he was studying. "I find her letters as entertaining as any play at Covent Garden."

"To your right." Lindsay motioned towards the upper portion of the huge desk. "With the others."

While the earl read, Mr. Sullivan shifted uneasily, his features becoming more forbidding than usual. "Cris," he began tentatively, "I realized when you gave me my position that it was only because you felt bound by family ties." His eyes began contemplating the intricacies of his shirt's pleating. "I appreciate all that you have done for me. I've always done my best to handle your affairs wisely. Now, however, I feel it is time for me to strike out on my own," he ended in a rush.

"Pardon me, Lin, I didn't hear you." Dunstan looked up from the marchioness's letter.

"I was saying . . . That is, it is time . . . Well, you have to find . . . find a new man to take my place."

"Whatever for? You haven't been cobbled by some wench who is pushing you into this, have you?" the surprised earl asked, leaning back, his eyes keenly upon his nervous, red-faced cousin.

"No, no one I would choose would have me," blurted Lindsay, his embarrassment complete.

"Now look, man, you're the best manager to be found. I'll double your wages . . ."

"No, Cris, listen. You've enabled me to make good investments. I've enough to buy my own land. Oh, nothing like Dunstan's Keep, but it will be my own," the young man said, regaining his composure. "I've been interviewing, discreetly, of course, and believe I have found the man to handle your estates."

Dunstan ran a finger tentatively along the line of his firm, square jaw. "You have been more than an agent. You've been a friend, Lin. I can only wish you well. This man you think capable . . ."

"Turrel," Sullivan supplied the name.

"Turrel. Could you have him settled in, say in two or three days?"

"Cris, my lord, I did not mean to leave you so abruptly."

"Can you do it?" Dunstan insisted.

"Yes, my lord." Lindsay straightened his striped lapels, his back rigid.

"Good. Hand over to him all matters concerning my land." He paused. "And do me the honour of re-

63

maining as my secretary until I return from one last excursion?"

"As you wish, my lord," Lin answered stiffly.

"You will need to travel with me this time," the earl pressed on with a smile, "for an extended stay in the country. An invitation from Aunt Philly," he pointed to the letter he had dropped upon his desk.

"But you haven't seen your aunt in"—he counted mentally—"in years." A pallour came over him. "Your mother . . . ?"

"Mother will present no problem."

"You may manage to handle her, Cris, but I would rather face a starving mob than Lady Dunstan when she has been crossed," Sullivan answered heatedly.

"Lin, you need to view Mother as someone with an unjust dun on my accounts. You handle that very well; apply it to Mother. Stop underrating yourself. Why, when I first asked you to take over my business matters, you were certain you couldn't handle them and yet you've managed a profit for me every year." The earl nodded, confirming a thought. "It is time you were more in society."

"A secretary rates attention from chambermaids and housekeepers, not from your set," Lin corrected him, flicking a piece of offending lint from his pantaloons.

"Your lack of title is no dishonour. Your blood is as good as mine. You yourself said you have your own means. Lady Phillippa and Lady Imogene will take you in hand, I am certain."

"We are to visit both your aunts?"

"No, all three. They are staying with . . . let me

see," his eyes flew over the letter, "with the Durhams at Braitlathe. Reverend Durham has two daughters, according to this, and Aunt Philly assures me they are most delectable."

" 'Pon my soul, no wonder Lady Dunstan has forbidden you to be familiar with her sisters."

"Calm yourself, Lin, that was my wording."

"Cris, I have never enjoyed travelling. I think it would be best if . . ."

"Oh, no. I need you. There are matters I must attend to during this visit and I need someone to . . . cover my absences."

"Not another . . . ? Cris, why don't you look about and settle on one petticoat? Surely it would be much easier to wed than to rush about the country chasing from one . . . well, doing as you do," Lin finished vaguely, disturbed by the annoyed look which had come over the earl's features at his words.

Dunstan studied his cousin and considered taking him into his confidence, but the danger such knowledge would place him in outweighed the urge.

"Was there something you would have me know?" Lin prompted.

"Affairs of the heart are personal, my friend . . . as you will one day come to know." The earl forced a laugh to his lips. "Now where do I sign these?" He waved a hand at the documents before him.

"Mother, I thought you had returned to the country. How well you look." Lord Dunstan bowed as he took her hand and kissed it.

"I am ghastly ill, far too ill to travel." Lady Dunstan sniffed into her lace kerchief as she gazed accusingly at her son.

"Doing it too brown, Mother. You haven't been ill a day in your life." The earl took a seat opposite the settee she lay upon. "Why are you still in London?"

Simpering having proved ineffective, Lady Dunstan turned to taking umbrage, and rose angrily. "How can you regard my health so nonchalantly?" she asked. "Why, Lord Brambye took his mother to Bath to partake of the waters simply because she sneezed."

"You would never consent to being seen in so unfashionable a place," her son teased.

"And Lord Naptel was faithfully at his mother's side during the entire season. But you," she continued undaunted, "you must be from one end of England to the other."

Patiently awaiting the end of her tirade, Dunstan showed little irritation. In fact, he smiled, causing his mother to drop her ploy.

"I thought you wished me wed," he noted innocently. "One must first court."

"Can you tell me the name of one marriageable miss you have encountered on these forays of yours? A miss who would be a fitting bride for the Dunstan name? None, I tell you. All eligible misses were here in London for the season," she replied sharply, then softened. "I have been thinking of having a summer party, a few of your friends . . ."

"I sincerely regret that I shan't be able to attend, Mother. Business matters call me away." He smiled.

"Business! Another light skirt. I don't mind your chasing after them, but can you not pause long enough to find a wife? I have introduced you to several . . ."

"Ghastly creatures," he ended for her. "Mother," he cautioned.

"But if only . . . You are already one and thirty," she said, changing tactics again. "Why, I shall go to the grave without seeing a grandchild." She sniffed, sitting upright.

Rising, Dunstan kissed her brow. "Never fear, Mother. I can always bring my by-blows to you," he teased.

"Oh, you are impossible, just as your father was." Her anger melted to sadness. "And I do love you as I did he."

"I know, Mother." Dunstan took her hand and gazed at her fondly. "And you have many days before you. Perhaps you may even see my heir and wheedle him into squiring you about."

"Oh, you *have* met someone! Is she eligible? When can I meet her?" Lady Dunstan gurgled excitedly.

"You shall meet her whenever I do," he smiled. "I have met no woman able to entice me to the altar. To bed, perhaps . . ." He winked.

"Wicked, wicked boy," Lady Dunstan scolded irritably. "Mind your tongue. Where are you off to this time?" she asked resignedly after a pause.

"To Braitlathe, a small village near Hastings. Lin is to go with me."

"I do wish you were more like your cousin. Just look at your toilet. Lin is always immaculate—and serious, as you properly should be but aren't."

"Lin is a good man," Dunstan agreed readily.

"But you should do something about his manner. Every time he is near me he squirms like a child who didn't eat all his porridge. But never mind. Why are you going to such a place?"

"Actually, Aunt Philly has invited me . . . and Aunt Imogene," he answered lightly.

"You mean they escaped Brienne?" Lady Dunstan asked scathingly. "You know I have forbidden you to see them."

"And I have not seen them for nine and ten years, Mother. I feel the need to renew family ties, and to see if my aunts are half as entertaining as their letters imply."

"I never could understand why you kept up correspondence with them. You were disobedient even at a tender age. I should have been forewarned of what you would become."

"I do everything you forbid, Mother."

"Phillippa will have some simpering miss she wishes to match you with. You wait and see. I have told you how her mind runs," she warned.

"Never fear, Mother. I have escaped your best-laid plots to ensnare me. Why should Aunt Philly be more successful? Till next we meet." Dunstan squeezed her hand and then bowed over it.

Lady Henrietta watched him go, pondering what her sisters, with whom she had neither spoken nor written to for years, could be scheming for her son.

"You are finished," Lady Brienne informed Deborah after the last portrait frame in the corridor had been dusted. "Lady Imogene promised to have tea ready beneath the oak."

"Yes, my lady." Deborah bobbed a curtsy and followed the baroness tiredly. Lady Brienne had proven a much sterner taskmistress than Sarita had ever been.

The ladies were barely settled in their chairs beneath the huge oak when Josh came running up to Lady Phillippa. "A rider just brought this, milady. Said I was to give it to you at once." He waved the letter in her face.

"Calm yourself, Josh," the marchioness said, finally catching hold of the missive. "Is the rider awaiting a reply?"

"No, milady. He left as soon as I told him you were here."

"That will be all." She dismissed him with a smile and broke the seal on the letter.

"Who is it from?" Lady Imogene asked excitedly.

"It is our answer, and as we expected," Lady Phillippa answered conspiratorially. Placing the letter carefully in her pocket, she picked up her cup and saucer. "Have you ever thought seriously of marriage, Sarita?" she asked, a matchmaking twinkle in her eye.

Chapter VII

Late June's bright morning sun was uncomfortably warm as Sarita hurried down the steps of the rectory. Her early morning tasks completed, she was rushing to Monsieur Mandel's greenhouse, where she helped with his work once or twice a week.

"Sarita! Oh, Sarita!" Lady Phillippa's voice halted her fast-paced steps. "My dear, are you going to Monsieur Mandel's?"

Turning, the young woman was confronted with the startling sight of the three dowagers. The countess's ample figure was swathed in a bright floral print, a huge spray of artificial flowers burdening the large straw hat upon her gray curls. Lady Brienne's toilet, very proper, was more subdued, being of a pale blue linen, but the hunting jacket style of the bodice and the tricorner hat atop her head couldn't help but draw eyes. A vivid green walking gown matched the spriteliness of the marchioness's spirit, and the long peacock feathers in her straw bonnet were a fitting touch.

"We shall accompany you to Monsieur Mandel's," the baroness told Sarita as the young woman dumbly nodded in reply. "Lead on, child. Tardiness is not a pleasant habit, especially for those who await you."

"Yes, my lady." Sarita forced her eyes from their

costumes, her surprise replaced by a bubble of laughter as she led the way.

"Parasols, ladies," Lady Brienne commanded as they followed.

"Yes, Brienne." The marchioness hurried forward to Sarita's side. "Walk with me, my dear," she said. "We wouldn't wish you to have too much sun."

"My complexion is far too darkened already for me to bother about the sun," she laughed.

" 'Tis true," Lady Imogene put in from behind them. " 'Haps your beaux don't care for milk and toast misses," she offered hopefully. "But I have heard that vinegar will whiten the skin."

"And lead arsenic also does," the baroness added. "Would you poison the child for your sport?"

"Oh, Brienne," the countess groaned.

"Don't worry, Sarita. Nothing so desperate as that will be necessary," Lady Phillippa assured her puzzled companion. "Now tell me about Monsieur Mandel's work. Does his son take part in it?"

"Does Monsieur Mandel approve of Napoleon?" asked Lady Imogene.

"Has there ever been gossip as to why Lord Peregrine allows them to stay?" Lady Brienne added.

"My ladies," Sarita's eyes twinkled mischievously, "it was my understanding that curiosity was a bane to gentle women."

"Respectful manners . . ." Lady Brienne began curtly.

"Come only after courteous questions," Sarita glanced back, not flinching. "As for the Mandels," she hurried on, "Monsieur Mandel is a loyalist, but totally immersed in his work with crossing strains of grains and vegetables. He never speaks of France, although it is my understanding he had extensive lands there.

"Pierre, I think, wishes to return to his home," she continued. "But he rarely speaks of Napoleon other than in polite murmurs of little meaning."

"And Lord Pergrine?" Lady Imogene asked again.

"When the Mandels first came, there was a rumour that Mandel was a count who had opened his home to Lord Pergrine years ago in France. Hence his lordship's present hospitality."

"Do you believe this?" the baroness questioned.

Sarita halted and faced her. "From what I know of Monsieur Mandel, I do not. I have seen him and Lord Pergrine together, and it appeared to me that they disliked each other intensely."

"It grows more interesting," Lady Phillippa noted.

"Yes, we must meet Lord Pergrine." Lady Imogene bobbed her flowered head.

"That shall be taken care of," Lady Brienne said confidently.

"My ladies." Sarita looked worriedly from one to the others. She had become fond of all three in the days since their arrival. "I ask you to heed a warning. Matters here are troubled. Do you not recall the murder we learned of your first day here? If you remain intent upon probing, I fear it will only bring you to harm. Father says . . ." she reconsidered the wisdom of her words and left them unspoken.

"Do not fear for us, Sarita." Lady Imogene patted her on the shoulder. "What need three old women such as we fear . . . or anyone fear from us? Your father is in much more danger than we."

"*Risque?* What is this you speak of?" Pierre Mandel appeared before them.

"We were just speaking of the unfortunate deaths that have occurred in the area," Lady Phillippa explained.

"Monsieur Mandel, we were hoping so much to see your father's greenhouses," Lady Imogene said, stepping forward. "Do you think it would be possible?"

"For such *mesdames charmantes* as yourselves, anything is possible." He smiled warmly at Sarita.

"Then you must escort us." Lady Phillippa took his arm.

"I shall attend your father," Sarita said and hurried off, his scowl following her.

"Monsieur Mandel," Lady Imogene tugged at his sleeve, "is that not one of the greenhouses behind those sycamores?"

"*Oui,*" he replied, forcing his attention back to the dowagers. "But it contains only the grain and vegetable plants. Would you rather see the *belles fleurs* that my father is working with this morn?" Mandel smiled enticingly.

"In good time, young man," the baroness answered. "For now the grain will do." She motioned him to proceed.

Glancing at the path down which Sarita had disappeared, Pierre summoned a warm smile to his haughty features and spewed copious compliments as he began an explanation of his father's work.

By the time they joined the elder Mandel and Sarita, it appeared the three dowagers had been entirely captivated by the young Frenchman's charms.

"Monsieur Mandel," Lady Imogene crooned, "such

a handsome son. So well-mannered, pleasingly different from many of our young Englishmen. You must be very pleased with him."

A flicker of distress crossed the elder Mandel's features.

"And so brilliant," the marchioness added her praise.

Shifting uneasily, Monsieur Mandel murmured, "*Merci.*" Father and son refused to look at one another.

"If you will excuse me, *mesdames,* Mademoiselle Durham, I have a matter I must attend to." Pierre bowed and strolled away without a word to his father.

"What beautiful flowers, Monsieur Mandel," Lady Phillippa filled the awkward silence. "Your work must be very enjoyable."

"*Oui.*" The bent, balding man brightened. "They are as my *enfants.*" He gazed lovingly over the bright array of blooms. "Every flower that blooms I have tried to gather together here."

"Is that not expensive?" Lady Brienne inquired.

"Lord Pergrine has been . . . most generous," Mandel replied, his features darkening. "But I have my own resources, and it is my hope to continue on my own soon." He smiled conspiratorily at Sarita. "With the prize money . . . But no, we must remain *sans paroles* on that. I have a rare lily in bloom." Mandel changed the direction of the conversation. "Follow me. I think you will find it most beautiful."

"Thank you so much, *monsieur,*" Lady Brienne

spoke for the three as the tour of the greenhouse ended.

"May we return?" the marchiness requested.

"At any time," he beamed. "Mademoiselle Durham's friends are most welcome. Good health, *mesdames,*" he said in farewell, returning to his work.

"We can find our way to the rectory, Sarita. There is no need for you to interrupt your work," the baroness told her. With brief parting words, the three women left.

Once away from the greenhouse, Lady Brienne halted. "We shall go to the main road."

"But that is much too far for us to walk," Lady Imogene protested, her round face already tinged with a hint of red from the morning's exertions.

"I had a most interesting conversation with that Mr. Conner, who called on Reverend Durham last eve. Come, if you wish to see what I learned."

"We may as well follow," Lady Phillippa told the countess, patting her encouragingly. "Brenny's simple-sounding whims usually have their own way of developing into something major."

"I wish she'd learn not to be so priggish about it," Lady Imogene countered.

"Come along, Immy. You know you shall," the marchioness cajoled her. "Tell me, what do you think his lordship, the Earl of Dunstan, will be like?"

"Knowing Henrietta, he could only be a dandy. I can see him, tall and thin as she and attired in some outlandish style current among the *ton.* His mother never did anything but mimic others."

"You shouldn't be so harsh, Immy. Henrietta has her good features. You know, she was even likeable after her marriage. How unfortunate that Lord Enoch died so young," the marchioness sighed. She had long regretted the breach between the sisters but saw little hope of reconciliation, since it had been caused by such a senseless rash of ill-timed occurrences that no one was any longer certain just why it had been brought about.

"Enoch," snorted the countess. "If I recall rightly, the lad was burdened with that dreadful name as well as a silver tray full of other names. What are they?" she asked as the two tramped along doggedly behind the baroness.

"Enoch Crispen Henry Edward Kennard, Earl of Dunstan," Lady Brienne tossed back.

"Didn't know you had taken such an interest in the lad," Lady Imogene taunted.

"Lad," hooted Lady Brienne. "At one and thirty? You are worse than his mother, wishing to keep him in swaddling, though I fear your judgment may prove true. While his letters oft have had the flavour of his father, Henrietta has more than likely had her way with his exterior. Be warned that Sarita will not take him if this proves true."

"Both of you should be ashamed," Lady Phillippa reproved them. "None of us has seen the lad . . . man"—she altered at the twitch of the baroness's eyebrow "—for many years. He has continued his correspondence with us in open defiance of his mother. Why should he not prove to be his own man in other matters as well?"

"Say what you will, Phillippa," said Lady Brienne. "I for one believe he will be meticulous in detail, foppish in dress, and uncertain in all other things," she pronounced in judgment. "But come along. If we tarry too long, we shall miss him."

"Who?" Lady Phillippa questioned as she hastened after her sister.

"You will see. Ah . . . I can hear the coach. Quickly now."

"Coach?" The countess exchanged a glance with Lady Phillippa.

"I told you she always knows more than she says. We had better bolt for the road."

The two joined Lady Brienne at the roadside just as a pair of high-stepping bays drawing a smartly appointed landau came into view.

Feigning a totally worn, frightened expression, the baroness fluttered her kerchief frantically in the air.

The short-bodied man in the landau reluctantly ordered his driver to halt as she stepped into the middle of the road.

"Oh, dear, kind sir," gushed the baroness, "how good of you to come to our rescue. We are horribly fatigued, and our footmen have not returned with our carriage. Help is so undependable in these times." A hand brushed tiredly across her brow. "Why, I told my sister, the Countess of Lackland," she motioned vaguely towards Lady Imogene, "that we simply must do something about them. But without the firm guidance of a man . . ." She sighed, letting the gentleman supply his own ending.

At the sound of the title, the bony, hawkish-faced wife came to attention. "Why, you would be the guests of Reverend Durham," she half-asked, leaning across her bulging husband for a closer look at the three.

"Unfortunately, yes," the baroness answered, her foot reaching Lady Phillippa's with enough force to stifle her defence of the Durhams. "One simply is not accustomed to such a household. Why, they have only one servant. Now I am a baroness and expect more discerning treatment."

"Then you must be the marchioness," the woman suddenly softened and stared at the three as if they were champion steeds. "You must repair to our estate at once. The Durhams cannot possibly be caring for you properly. We shall." Her pride in having three such titled trophies gracing her home and upcoming ball, for the envy of all the local gentry, showed plainly.

"Anne, we haven't . . ."

"Never fear, sir," the baroness said haughtily. "We do not habitate just any home."

"A thousand pardons, my ladies," Lady Pergrine fluttered a hand at them. "Let us introduce ourselves. My husband, Viscount Pergrine. I insist that you come to our home. It must be ghastly for you, what with Mrs. Durham's . . ."

"Your invitation is most gracious and sincerely appreciated, but there are times when one must decline such offers. Sacrifice for a better good, you understand. Reverend Durham is, after all, a minister," Lady Brienne noted stiffly. "And we have a nephew, the Earl of Dunstan, coming soon who shall expect to find us with the Durhams."

"It would be a vast relief, however, if we could feel free to call on you," Lady Phillippa spoke for the first time.

"Oh, yes, do so. At any time, my ladies. I know

several women whose company I am certain you would enjoy. Perhaps you could come to tea on Thursday next? And you must consider coming to our ball. Lord Gerard is coming for a visit shortly, you know."

"That sounds delightful," Lady Phillippa told her, flashing her warmest smile. "And of course you shan't object if Mrs. Durham and her daughters accompany us? I just dread awkward situations."

"Why . . . I . . . don't . . ." Lady Pergrine looked with dismay to her husband.

" 'Tis no matter," he grunted, eyeing Lady Brienne with a curious intensity. "Don't be giving such open invitations again," Pergrine whispered the command. Turning to the dowagers, he tipped his hat.

Before his lordship could order his driver on, Lady Imogene stepped forward. "Why, Lord Pergrine, I don't know what we should have done had you not come along. We had lost our way, and our naughty footmen have not returned for us. How kind of you to take us back to Braitlathe," she continued, her hand firmly upon the landau's door.

"Why . . . why, of course. We shall take you back to Malvern's Manor, or so it is called by most," Lady Pergrine prattled, ignoring her husband's scowl.

The bays turned about, Pergrine ordered the driver to use his whip. The landau slowed as it neared the place where the dowagers' coach had been disabled.

Grabbing hold of their hats as the driver veered his team off the road, the startled trio were jounced over stones and large limbs before finding themselves once again on the rutted path.

Lady Pergrine twittered apologetically. "The bog,"

she motioned behind them. "Only strangers try to manage it unless it be thoroughly dry. I have told Lord Pergrine that the road should be diverted about it, but it is such an expense and everyone knows to avoid it."

Chapter VIII

"This cannot be the way," Lin Sullivan fretted. "We have seen no one for hours." Lin readjusted his lace jabot as they jostled down the rutted road.

"We left Pordean only a few hours past," Lord Dunstan returned. "Enjoy the countryside."

"There," Sullivan pointed, "there is a path, Cris." Lin looked back as they passed it. "It was the only one we've seen."

"Didn't look wide enough for the phaeton. You wouldn't want us tipping over, would you?"

"Oh, no." Lin's glance sought assurance that Dunstan was joking. The journey thus far had firmed his conclusion that he was indeed a pitiable traveller, for being bounced at breakneck speeds over bad roads had proven wearying to him, while his cousin had laughed at the discomfort and revelled at being in the open air.

"I think mayhap we shall go on to Runnet before going to Braitlathe," Dunstan thought aloud. "Might be best to establish . . ."

"Mayhap we shall even go on to Hastings," Sullivan snorted. "To speak with more of your unusual acquaintances. I never realized what odd friends you have acquired, Cris."

"To Hastings it is, if you wish," Dunstan tossed

back with a wide smile, hoping Lin would forget those odd friends.

"Cris, look ahead. I believe you had better halt," Sullivan warned, seeing the suspicious morass before them. "Cris . . ." a huge rut ended his words as he grabbed hold of the phaeton's side to keep his seat.

The blacks reached the midpoint of the mire with only slight trouble but bogged down as the phaeton sank beyond axle depth.

"Now what are we to do? We're surrounded by . . . mud," Lin noted with a cringe. "How are we to get beyond this?"

"By walking," Dunstan told him cheerfully.

"*Through* it?"

"Of course. It brings to mind Old Nanny, shuddering at the sight of me coated with mud from head to foot. I hesitate to recall Mother's words," laughed the earl as he quieted his team.

"Actually *walk* in it . . . You *do* mean it." Lin looked at him aghast.

"Have you never had a good romp in the mud?" Dunstan feigned shock while inwardly staving off the laughter his cousin's consternation was brewing. Lin's fastidiousness had long been a tolerated bane to the earl, and he could not help teasing his cousin. "You certainly will have that romp now, for one of us must get yon branch and place it beneath the axle if we are to be free of this bog."

Lin surveyed his own impeccable dress—mauve pantaloons and matching long coat with yellow lapels. He ran a hand carefully over his meticulously tied cravat and then took in the earl's buckskin breeches and comfortably worn coat, which he had been travelling in from the beginning of the journey. Each day Lin had hoped to see at least a waistcoat added or something other than the plain linen shirt, devoid of lace or even tucks. The wish had been in vain, his lordship donning a clean, equally simple shirt each day, and today even the cravat, which Dunstan usually looped disdainfully about his neck, was absent.

The earl, plainly enjoying himself, leaned back in the seat. "You had best see to that branch if we are to go on."

His cousin drew himself up. Staring straight ahead, he said in clipped tones, "Not I."

"But I am the earl," Dunstan said, feigning injured protest. "How can my dignity allow me to venture into the mire?" He waved a hand theatrically.

"Your title did not prevent you from wrestling with the innkeeper's son at Tunbridge Wells. Besides, you are stronger." Lin brightened at this thought. "You did win the match."

Laughing at his cousin's seriousness, Dunstan handed him the reins. "Think how valuable a secretary you must be that an earl is willing to remove you from a bog. Mayhap you wish me to carry you free of it?" he joked.

Sullivan blushed furiously, a hurt expression in his eyes.

"Lin, I am sorry for plaguing you," his lordship assured him contritely. "We both know I will be happier doing it. Many a time I have thought you better suited to the title." He paused, then seriousness fled. "My sense of nobility is abhorrently lacking." He shook his head in mock sadness and vaulted from the phaeton into the morass.

"You may yet learn some degree of dress," Lin told him in all seriousness. "Truly, Cris, you have the makings of an excellent peer, if only you would attain some degree of decorum."

"Let us be glad for now that I have none," the earl shot back, slogging toward dry ground.

Sarita had gone on an errand collecting plants for Monsieur Mandel from various gardens in the area, and her long walk led her to the main road. She tramped along, gently swinging the basket of plants and humming a gay ditty. The sounds of a man's shouts and a team's straining caused her to leave off her tune and hurry forward. Not the bog again, she thought with a frown, realizing she was near it. A loud snap sounded, then a dull plop, followed by a burst of unrestrained laughter as she neared the phaeton.

"I fear you shall have to strain yourself, my lord," she heard a deep, hearty voice proclaim and realized it emanated from the mud-coated hulk rising from the mire behind the phaeton.

Lin, who had stood up to see the earl's fate when the branch he was using for leverage snapped, was still taking in his thoroughly muddied cousin as Sarita came upon them. Raising his eyes, he encountered her small form as she hesitantly approached.

"Thank God," Lin heaved a sigh of relief. "Miss! Oh, miss!" He waved at her to come closer. "Fetch your father or brothers to come aid us."

Halting at the edge of the mud, unconsciously raising her skirts to keep them clean, she stared at the man within. A pair of laughing eyes met her own, ran down her figure, and ended appreciatively on her neatly turned ankles. He gave an elaborate bow, and she could not help bursting into laughter at the ludicrous sight he presented.

"Cris, mind your ways," Lin chortled, fearing his salvation was being tampered with. "I apologize, miss."

"That is quite unnecessary, my lord." She bobbed a tardy curtsy, and smiled at the mud-covered hulk before her. *What deep, brown eyes he has*, she thought. An odd sensation stirred within her beneath his half-humourous, half-serious gaze.

"We shall need your husband's aid," the mud-daubed gentleman spoke, enjoying his scrutiny of the petite figure before him.

"I have no husband, and my father is not at home," she replied, feeling her cheeks grow warm beneath his stare.

"Surely there is someone," Lin said again as the pair gazed at each other without speaking. "Cris, you must do something."

Dunstan shrugged, his eyes full of mirth. "Do you think we could get his lordship to dry land . . . spotless, of course?" he asked Sarita, attempting to keep his tone grave.

"Cris!" Lin's distress increased at Dunstan's deliberate mistake in addressing him.

"What am I to do with his lordship?" the earl reiterated, emphasizing the title and turning to face Lin with a threatening look.

"Can you not manage to reach one of the team's backs?" Sarita offered. "Then the horses could be unhitched and led to dry ground."

"A capital idea," Dunstan agreed.

Scowling, Sullivan glared at him. "*You* would think so."

"A little horse hair never hurt anyone," he consoled his cousin.

"Why, my lord, you are sitting on it," Sarita offered, then blushed at the audacity of her words.

Dunstan let loose a bark of laughter, which increased her consternation and his cousin's. Turning to Lin, he wiped his hand on the inside of his jacket and offered to assist him. With Sarita looking on, the earl managed to get his cousin a-horse and lead him free.

Slipping to the ground with obvious relief, Lin bowed to Sarita and noticed that his lordship couldn't seem to take his eyes from her. "Pardon me, miss. Miss . . ." He gained her attention. "Would you know the direction of Braitlathe?"

"Of course. I live there." She smiled over his shoulder at Dunstan.

"Are you one of the Misses Durham?" Lin asked in surprise.

"Why, yes." He had her full attention now. "But how did you know?"

"Lady Bawden . . ."

"You are the Earl of Dunstan!" Sarita clapped a hand over her mouth, taking in Lin's appearance and swallowing a chortle of laughter. "I should have known." She waved a hand, taking in the mauve jacket with the yellow lapels. "Your . . . bearing," she ended weakly and blushed furiously as the muddied hulk behind Lin let loose a fresh burst of mirth.

"You are mistaken, miss. I am . . ." Sullivan began, completely flustered by her error.

"His lordship, Lord Enoch here, has to be forgiven." Dunstan stepped to Lin's side and reached an arm around his cousin's shoulders.

Sullivan shied from him like a skittish colt.

"It has been a difficult day for his lordship. Do you think we could be going to Braitlathe now, Miss Durham?"

Sarita wondered at the mischievous glint in the man's eyes. Why did she feel he was maneuvering a trick of some sort? What a strangely personal relationship between him and the earl, she thought; not at all as she would have imagined an earl would wish to be treated. But then, she concluded, this was not so strange when one thought of the dowagers. "My home is not far from here, Mr. . . . ?"

"Sullivan. Chris Sullivan at your service, miss." The earl gave an elaborate bow.

A choking cough claimed their attention. Sarita hurried to Lin's side and began thumping him on the back with all her strength.

"His lordship has these spells," Dunstan assured her. "He'll be fine once we arrive at Braitlathe, and he can rest."

"Fine?" Lin choked out. "I . . . was . . . fine . . . until I came on this journey."

"Before we go, Mr. Sullivan, you might wish to wash in the stream just beyond," Sarita said, studying the two. "If you are quite recovered, my lord, I will show him the way."

"You wait here, my lord." The earl bowed to his cousin with a wink. "I'll not tarry long."

"Let me have your coat," Sarita ordered crisply when they reached the stream.

Surprised, Dunstan nevertheless shucked the muddy disaster from his broad shoulders.

"You had best be washing off," she urged him. " 'Tis no small chore," she added, taking in the muscular shoulders beneath the plain linen shirt as he waded into the stream. Stooping at the edge, Sarita dropped the coat into the water and began scrubbing it.

"But you will soil your gown," Dunstan protested.

"I have managed to do that before," she laughingly told him. "Not quite as well as you have done, however."

Dunstan joined in her laughter and began to rid himself of the drying muck. The task completed as well as he was able without disrobing, he returned to the bank. Halting where Sarita was still stooped over, brushing at his devastated coat, he eyed her trim figure carefully.

"It has not fared well, I fear," she said, looking up.

He reached down and took her hand, drawing her upright. Her head barely reached his chest. " 'Tis a small matter," Dunstan said softly, and her heart raced at the caress of his voice.

"Cris? Cris, where are you? Will you never be done?" Lin's nervous voice reached their ears.

"Ah, peers," he sighed, and winked at Sarita. Grabbing his coat deftly from the ground, he guided her back to the team. "Shall you ride, my lord?" he asked his cousin.

Lin grimaced. "I choose to walk. Miss Durham?" He held out his hand to her.

"My basket?" She turned back to where she had set it down.

"Mr. Sullivan may fetch it," Lin assured her haughtily, feeling he was attaining a small degree of revenge for Cris's prank.

With regret, she placed her hand upon his arm and led the way, glancing back and wondering why her heart hammered so as the very damp Mr. Sullivan winked at her.

Chapter IX

"The ladies will be having tea," Sarita told the man she believed to be the earl as they neared the rectory.

"An unusual home, Miss Durham," Dunstan noted from behind the two. "Where shall our chambers be?" he asked, surveying the towers.

"The tower room on the right has a large bed-chamber with a smaller attached room. I think you shall be comfortable there, Mr. Sullivan." Sarita flashed a smile over her shoulder. "The stable is there." She pointed it out. "Josh will take care of the horses for you."

For a moment, basking in her smile, the earl forgot the reason for his question. Giving himself a mental shake, he surveyed the tower in question. A large trellis reached to the upper floor and vining covered most of the east side above it. A smile came to his lips as he noted the large stone ledge beneath the windows, marking the upper floor from the lower. His chamber would be most accessible.

"Shall we not enter properly?" Lin asked nervously as Sarita led them from the path towards the rear of the house.

"But we always take tea out of doors," Sarita told him. "The ladies will think it odd if I do not bring you to them at once. They have been quite excited at the prospect of your visit."

"It is most irregular." Lin refused to go forward.

"What is more odd? My being unchaperoned with two gentlemen all afternoon, or tea outdoors?" she asked exasperatedly.

"Oh, dear," Lin exclaimed, aghast. "I never thought. I mean . . ." He wrung his hands fretfully.

"Well, old man," Dunstan said, rejoining the two. "Looks like you will wed at last. Compromising this little lady. Tsk, tsk." His eyes sparkled as he gauged Sarita's reaction.

"M-married," his cousin stammered. "Cris, now, Cris, you know . . ."

"Mr. Sullivan teases, my lord," Sarita assured him, undecided whether or not to be annoyed at the one's boldness or the other's trying nervousness. "Let us join your aunts, my lord." She frowned a reprimand at Mr. Sullivan as she spoke.

"Sarita, my dear, we were becoming concerned." Mrs. Durham rose at her daughter's approach. "Why, whom do you have with you?" She smiled at Lin's immaculate appearance and frowned at the earl's dismal state.

"Mother, this is the dowagers' nephew, the Earl of Dunstan."

Mrs. Durham fell into a deep curtsy. "My lord," she said in greeting.

"And this is his . . ."

"Personal secretary," Dunstan supplied.

"Mr. Sullivan," Sarita ended, finding herself unaccountably brightening to learn that he was not his lordship's valet.

"Rise, please rise," Lin besought the rector's wife,

reaching out and drawing her upright. "This is not necessary at all. Actually there has been a misunderstanding . . ."

"Yes, his lordship drove us into the center of a bog," Dunstan interrupted smoothly. "My appearance has suffered somewhat in the attempt to remove the phaeton and I do apologize for it." He bowed, bringing a glimmer of approval to Mrs. Durham's features.

At mention of the quagmire, Lady Imogene and Lady Phillippa rose and approached the group.

"Perhaps you know of someone who can assist in the freeing of Lord Dunstan's phaeton?" the earl continued.

"Your Mr. Traunt, Sarita," Lady Phillippa offered and noted Mr. Sullivan's sharp glance at the young woman. "Could he not aid Mr. Sullivan as he did us? And you must be Lord Enoch." The marchioness turned to Lin without waiting for Sarita's reply. "So pleased to see you once again." She mentally shook her head at his foppish attire.

"I . . . I, also," Lin stammered, bright red spots coming to his cheeks at the deceit he was being forced to continue.

"I am Lady Phillippa, dear Enoch." The marchioness raised on tiptoe as she stepped near him and brushed his cheek with a kiss.

"And I am the Countess of Lackland," Lady Imogene told him, thinking how unfortunate Henrietta's success had been with the young man. "Your Aunt Imogene."

"Steady, man," Dunstan whispered, taking his cousin's arm as signs of bolting crossed Lin's features.

"And you must be Lady Brienne." The earl nodded

while keeping hold of Sullivan. "His lordship has spoken highly of you."

"Has he no tongue to speak on his own?" she bristled.

Given a push by the earl, Lin had no choice but to move forward. A look told him that Dunstan was serious in maintaining the misunderstanding about their respective identities. "Forgive me." He brushed a lace-edged cuff across his brow. "The excitement of the accident and now meeting all of you for the first time . . . in many years," he added hastily and posed affectedly.

Behind him Dunstan's smile grew. His cousin was more adept than he had hoped.

Watching the interplay, Sarita again had a feeling of doubt, the oddest sense that Mr. Sullivan was enjoying a huge joke.

"Lady Brienne, why such a frown?" Sarita asked as the baroness stalked into the dining salon bearing the supper plates.

Setting them down with a clanking thud, she replied, "Lord Dunstan."

"What has his lordship done?" Sarita winced as her mother's best plates were roughly slammed into place. "I shall finish this for you." She took the last four. "He could not have had time to . . ."

"He can. He is Henrietta to the core. Our sister, you know. I find it hard to believe he has ever stood up to her."

"Perhaps he will make a better impression as he becomes more familiar with all of you," Sarita offered hopefully.

"I warned Imogene and Phillippa. I told them what would happen. It will be a disappointment, my dear, if you choose to . . ."

"Yes, Lady Brienne?"

"Never mind. Has that Mr. Sullivan returned?" the baroness asked, changing the topic of discussion.

"Yes," Sarita laughed lightly. "Tessy put him to work carrying water for his own bath. He seemed a bit taken aback at having to do it, though." She paused.

"Do you like Mr. Sullivan?"

"I see nothing to dislike in the man, barring his familiarity at times." Sarita shrugged off the question. "He is very different from Lord Dunstan."

"Everyone is different from his lordship, thank the Lord. I think I shall speak with Mr. Sullivan about providing us with some extra servants, however . . . so his lordship can be properly cared for." She rolled her eyes.

"You couldn't . . . I mean you wouldn't. Father would . . ."

"What is this I am to do?" Reverend Durham asked, startling Sarita with his unexpected entry.

"Good eve, Father." She greeted him with a kiss after recovering. "Did you not go to the solarium? We have more guests this eve."

"I know. Our stable is nigh to overflowing, and these last are prime blood."

"My nephew, Lord Dunstan, has arrived, Reverend Durham," Lady Brienne told him. "At least he knows his horseflesh, and business matters. Unusually well for a peer, though," she mused aloud. "I had better fetch the water goblets," the baroness continued, sensing that the rector wished to speak alone with his daughter.

When the door closed, concern aged his features. "How are we to go on?" he asked. "With all these guests? Can you manage the work?"

"I have done well with the dowagers' help, Father. And late this afternoon a haunch of beef was brought to the door, along with other staples, compliments of the earl, according to the boys who brought the items."

"Most unusual." He rubbed his forehead. "I suppose we had best thank the Lord and not question the source," he concluded uneasily. "Does his lordship have a pleasing demeanour?"

"He is very proper," Sarita returned carefully.

"Sarita . . . Sarita!" Deborah burst into the salon. "Have you seen him? Oh!" She halted abruptly. "Good eve, Father." She brushed his cheek with a kiss and turned to her sister. "Isn't he superb? Didn't I tell you that the ladies would help us," she continued in her excitement. "We may not even have to go to London to make a match." Recalling her father standing behind her, Deborah gulped in dismay.

"I shall have to meet this paragon." The rector's deep voice was tinged with humour, his brows arched and his eyes twinkling. "I shall bring our guest in to sup after I have assessed him," he told them and walked solemnly from the chamber.

"Oh, Sarita." Deborah collapsed into a chair. "I thought I would receive a terrible scold," she said in relief. "Why do you suppose I did not?" She sat up.

Her sister shrugged nonchalantly. "You truly like the earl?"

"He is the most marvelous creature I have ever seen. The first earl I have ever met," she sighed. "Did you not take note of his jacket? No one has such garments here."

"I am certain of that."

Deborah eyed her sister suspiciously, but was forestalled from making a retort by the baroness's return.

"Go to the kitchen," they were ordered. "Tessy and Imogene have everything ready. I hope Lord Enoch doesn't have an apoplexy when he sees there is no one to serve us." She clucked as she set the tray of goblets on the table.

"Oh, Sarita, couldn't Tessy serve us? Please?" Deborah begged.

"The earl will survive," her sister answered dryly.

"But what shall he think of us?" Distress filled her features.

Taking her arm, Sarita guided her sister towards the door. "I could ask him if you wish."

"Oh . . . you!" Deborah shook free of the hold and stalked off.

Looking back to the baroness, Sarita arched her brows. "His lordship is not without talent; he has already made one conquest."

"But not the one planned."

"What do you mean?"

"Good eve, ladies." The earl came lithely into the dining salon. "Mrs. O'Neal said you would direct me?" He raised the pitcher of water in his hand.

"I am sorry, Mr. Sullivan," Sarita apologized as she hurried forward. "You are not expected to serve . . ."

Dunstan raised the pitcher from her reach. "I dare not raise Mrs. O'Neal's ire," he noted seriously.

"Those goblets, Mr. Sullivan," the baroness interceded. "You had best fill them. Hurry to the kitchen, Sarita. It wouldn't do to alarm his lordship by having him seated before you return."

Frowning at her defeat, Sarita controlled her urge to kick the grinning Mr. Sullivan in the shins and left.

"Have you been with Lord Enoch long, young man?" Lady Brienne scrutinized him carefully.

"Five years, my lady," he answered as he poured the water.

"And you handle all his affairs?"

"No, my lady, only those he wishes me to," Dunstan said, intent upon his work.

"Mayhaps you need a lesson in respect, Mr. Sullivan?"

"I've no doubt you could give it, my lady." The earl looked directly at her. "But Lord Dunstan's concerns, business or otherwise, are his."

Reading the strength of the man, the baroness smiled. "He is to be commended in his selection of confidants," she retreated gracefully. "Sullivan? Of the Hertfordshire Sullivans? Aren't you connected with the Dunstans?"

"Yes, my lady. The earl and I are second cousins." He assessed her more closely.

Their conversation was ended by Sarita and Deborah's return and the entry shortly afterwards of the remainder of the family and guests.

"How long shall you be staying with us, Lord Dunstan?" Reverend Durham asked an hour later as all relaxed after Tessy had brought dessert to the table.

Lin looked nervously at Dunstan.

"His lordship's schedule is quite flexible at this time," the earl answered. "We look forward to an extended stay. Lord Dunstan hopes to meet Lord Pergrine while we are here." The coldness which fell over the room caught him totally unprepared. Sweeping over those about the table, his eyes settled upon Sarita, who met his gaze with questioning accusation.

"It is rather late," Lin stammered apprehensively. "Mayhap we should adjourn for port now?"

"An excellent idea, Lord Dunstan," Reverend Durham quickly agreed. "It has been a long day for us all. A bit of spirits will relax us for an early retiring. We are to have a military drill on the meadow at first light. I do hope it shall not disturb you unduly," he said, rising.

"Pardon, Reverend Durham," Tessy said, entering the dining salon hesitantly. "That young Mr. Mandel is here, wishin' ta see Miss Sarita."

All eyes swung to her, but she felt Mr. Sullivan's the keenest.

"Sarita?" her father questioned.

"Did Monsieur Mandel mention his reason for calling?" she asked Tessy.

"No, miss. He did ask if his lordship, Lord Dunstan"—she nodded towards Lin—"was to be stayin' at Malvern."

"Perhaps he might be willing to join us all in the solarium," Dunstan suggested lightly.

"Monsieur Mandel is such a charming young man, I should regret missing the opportunity of visiting with him again," Lady Brienne put in, curious to learn of young Mandel's interest in the earl and Mr. Sullivan's interest in the Frenchman.

"Tessy, show Mr. Mandel to the solarium and then fetch port for the gentlemen," Reverend Durham ordered.

When all were assembled in the solarium, Pierre Mandel approached the rector. "I apologize for intruding," he began.

"You are welcome in our home, Mr. Mandel," the rector cut him off gently. "How fares your father?" he asked, forcing himself to be pleasant.

"*Très bien, merci.* And you, Mrs. Durham?" He turned to the rector's wife and bowed over her hand. "I see you are in the best of looks, as usual," he smiled.

"Why, thank you, Mr. Mandel," she fluttered.

"And you, Mademoiselle Durham, exquisite as always." Pierre reached to take Sarita's hand, but she avoided him.

"Tessy said you wished to speak with me, Monsieur Mandel?" she asked.

"*Oui.* Father wishes you to come to the greenhouse early in the morn. The project is near its time," he told her smoothly.

"So soon? But I thought it would be . . ."

"I simply bring the message," the arrogant young man shrugged.

"Of course. Tell your father I shall come," she answered, still puzzled. Monsieur Mandel had assured her only that morn that it would be some time before his secret project would be ready.

"Perhaps the *mesdames* would like to come also,"

Pierre continued. "And your other guests." He bowed towards Lin and Dunstan, who had entered the solarium last.

"My lord," Reverend Durham stepped to Mandel's side, "may I present Pierre Mandel, a neighbor. Pierre, this is Mr. Sullivan and Lord Kennard, Earl of Dunstan."

Giving an elaborate bow, Pierre murmured greetings. "Will you be staying long, my lord?" he asked.

"I . . . I really do not know. It depends upon what I . . . find here," Lin replied nervously.

"Think 'dun'," Dunstan whispered to his cousin as he sauntered to one side.

"Your accent is French, Mr. Mandel. May we presume you are originally from France?" Lin asked, his composure in hand for the first time that evening.

"*Oui*. I was displaced by the First Consul's decree," Pierre answered, his voice hardening. "I believe you support the war effort, *n'est-ce pas?*"

"Naturally," Lin answered, affronted, and then launched into a speech on the economic ramifications of the war between the two countries.

"My ladies." The baroness held court in her chamber. "What are we to do? Lord Enoch will not suit Sarita."

"He has been here but a half day," Lady Imogene protested. "He handled himself quite well with that young Mr. Mandel."

Lady Brienne bowed. "Well, but dully. Enoch is too much like Henrietta. You cannot saddle Sarita with such a man for life."

"Lord Enoch may have faults," Lady Phillippa

joined the conversation, "but let us wait a few days before passing judgment. He may simply be shy among strangers."

"I imagine that is why he keeps Mr. Sullivan so close," Lady Imogene agreed.

"There is something about Mr. Sullivan . . . and I mean more than his manner," the baroness noted. "Did either of you notice anything?"

"Of course not, Brienne," the countess dismissed the idea. "It is only that he is a personable young man."

"Yes, wouldn't it be perfectly wonderful if we could interest him in Deborah?" the marchioness beamed.

"Hruummph!" came from Lady Brienne.

"Sarita, what do you think of him?" Deborah asked, as the sisters readied for bed.

"Who?"

"Don't tease, Sarry. Lord Enoch."

"His lordship is . . . fair featured." She found a safe compliment at last.

"He is the handsomest man I have ever seen," Deborah sighed. "And so fashionably attired."

"He is an earl," Sarita tried to caution her sister, "and not likely to take note of a rector's daughter."

"We shall see." Deborah plopped onto her bed. "I believe you are jealous because he looked at me twice during supper." Deborah hugged her pillow close. "Such deep blue eyes, and an earl . . . Imagine, Sarita, an earl." She sighed.

Listening to her sister's babbling, Sarita dropped onto her bed. Deborah's ravings would remain humourous only so long as the earl remained uninterested. Would he play loose with a naive young girl's feelings? She drifted to sleep, her thoughts dwelling on the twinkling brown eyes and hearty laugh of the earl's secretary.

"Cris, you have gone mad at last. What can you mean by this?" Lin was pacing to and fro, having failed to persuade the earl to reveal his true identity in the morning. "We must explain . . ." he began again.

"That is impossible just yet," Dunstan cut him off. "Not that I don't mean to clarify matters," he went on. "Bear with me. It is important."

Lin arched his brows in disbelief. "And what am I to do about your aunts, especially Lady Brienne? You would not believe her questions." He daubed at his forehead with his lace-edged kerchief.

"You can always plead ignorance. After all, it has been many years since you have seen her. Explain that mother never mentioned them or their family, or whatever she is asking after. You can manage it."

"But what of Lord Pergrine? Are you not acquainted with him?"

"We met briefly a few years past. I see no problem with him." Dunstan removed his coat and began undoing his cravat, donned in honour of supper with the Durhams. "Did you notice the effect the mention of his name produced?"

"There is more than one strange apple about. What of this Mandel? He is an odd one with his perfumed lace," Lin ended cryptically.

Dunstan arched his brow at this comment but did not speak. "We had best be to bed, Lin," he said finally. "If Reverend Durham is to drill the home militia in the morn, I doubt we shall sleep much past first light. They may be short on skill, but I suspect they are long on shouting." He placed a hand on his cousin's shoulder. "I would not ask this of you if it were not important."

Studying the earl's features, more serious and intent than Lin had ever seen them, he wondered if the man were more complex than he supposed. "All right, Cris, but your explanation had bloody well be good."

Dunstan nodded.

"Which chamber shall you take?" Lin looked about hesitantly.

"You shall have the smaller," the earl smiled. "I shall explain it, if the matter is noticed, by telling them you are fearful of fresh air." He motioned to the surrounding windows.

With a knowing frown, Lin bowed and went to his room.

Later, abed, Dunstan went over Mandel's conversation with Lin. Something about the Frenchman troubled him. The nagging question was replaced by a far different picture as he drifted off to sleep—the vision of a petite miss energetically scrubbing his mud-daubed coat.

Chapter X

Barked orders, shouts, and the clamour of confusion
awakened Lin Sullivan early the next morning.
Grumbling at the disturbance, he arose to pull the
windows down. This having no effect on the ca-
caphony, he stumbled into the earl's larger room.
"Don't see why they have to make such a confounded
din." He slammed a window down. "Hasn't it awakened you?" When no response came, Lin tramped to
the large, canopied bed. Jerking back the covers, he
was shocked to discover that the bed was empty.
"Now where could he have gone," he mumbled, a
hand tousling his hair. A thought took him to the
windows, where he carefully scrutinized the rugged
band of men drilling in the meadow. Most wore the
garb of common farmers, and a few showed evidence
of being more prosperous in their unpatched coats,
but none resembled his cousin.

Watching the attempted maneuvers, Lin considered
returning to bed, then saw a fat, short-bodied man
atop a blood stallion gallop up to the men and rear
his mount to a halt before the leader. Too far away
to hear what was spoken, he recognized anger in the
gestures of the mounted man, whose dress bespoke
the quality. "Why, the man is raging at Reverend
Durham," Lin said aloud, shocked.

The rector was standing stolidly, enduring the harangue. The men about the two, however, began separating and moving back.

"Why doesn't someone go to the man's defense?" slipped indignantly from Lin's lips. Alarm followed as a band of horsemen broke from the woods. At first glance, Sullivan took them for brigands, for many had pistols in their waistbands and carried shooting pieces as well.

"Cris, where are you?" he bemoaned his more daring cousin's absence. "You would know what to do." A motion from the first mounted man caught his eye. To his amazement the approaching men reined to a halt. The first then signaled towards the rapidly retreating home militia, whose weapons Sullivan now saw were merely sticks of wood. Acknowledging the sign, the men spurred to drive the troop farther away. A final barrage of words was let loose on Durham, and then the mounted man followed his men. The rector stood staring stiffly after them. Slowly his shoulders sagged, and he plodded towards the rectory.

Fully awake, Lin rushed to his chambers, pulling off his nightdress as he went. A quiet thudding and then a gentle but insistent tapping in the earl's chamber interrupted his hurried dressing. Curiously, cautiously, he stepped into the chamber. The tapping grew louder. Lin's mouth gaped at the sight of Lord Dunstan clinging to the vining outside the window.

"Good lord!" He rushed forward and wrenched the window open. "Cris, what are you trying to do?"

"To come in, my man, to come in—which I could have done unaided if you had not closed the windows," Dunstan quipped as he swung his legs inside.

"Did you see what happened in the meadow?" Lin

asked excitedly as the earl stood up. "I thought that ruffian was going to attack Reverend Durham."

"The ruffian was Lord Pergrine," Dunstan clipped as he shrugged out of his damp coat. "Now we know why his name was so coldly received last eve," he said as he tossed his coat into the wardrobe and removed another. Laying it on his bed, he sat down and motioned for his cousin to help remove his boots.

"Did you hear what was said?" Lin asked as he straddled the earl's leg and began tugging.

"I was too far away and dared go no closer. Something about the men drilling with Durham, I think."

The boot popped free. Dropping the distasteful object, Lin faced his cousin. "What were you doing out there?"

"In good time, Lin, you will know it all, believe me. For now it is best you remain ignorant, and"—a warning look was cast at him—"say nothing of my comings and goings." He motioned toward the open window. "Also, please do not shut my windows." He raised his other leg, motioning at his boot. "It could prove most embarrassing if I were forced to enter by way of the Misses Durham's chamber."

Sullivan dropped the second boot and brushed his hands free of the damp blades of grass. "I am becoming wiser, Cris. You say that merely to tease me," he returned haughtily.

A light knock prevented reply. Stocking-footed, Dunstan went to the door.

"Good morn, Mr. Sullivan," Lady Phillippa greeted him cheerfully. "Breakfast will be served in a few moments."

"Is it not early for you to be up, my lady?" the earl asked. "His lordship is . . ."

"You will simply have to wake Enoch." She patted his arm. "Breakfast is served but once in this household. To miss it is to do without, no matter what your rank," she added for his benefit. "We thought it best Enoch learn this at once. Hopefully it will prevent future grief for us all," she sighed. Edging forward conspiratorially, the marchioness whispered, "I do hope this will not cause Lord Enoch to bolt for London. It would be regrettable for him . . . and for you as well," she smiled.

"For me?" the earl asked innocently.

"Why, yes, Mr. Sullivan. Do I dare believe you have failed to take note of Reverend Durham's daughters?" Lady Phililppa asked artlessly. "Although little good it may do you. Both young ladies have many admirers. Well, no more on that. Remember, breakfast now, or do without."

Chuckling, Lord Dunstan closed the door.

"What kind of a household is this?" Lin choked out. "Do they not know the kind of treatment a peer deserves?"

"You forget 'your' aunts are peeresses." Dunstan smiled broadly.

Moving to the mirror on the large wardrobe, Lin began working meticulously on the folds of his cravat. "Breakfast will be served only once," he mimicked the marchioness.

"Why, cousin, I didn't know you had such a gift," the earl laughed.

"Nor did I realize that entering upper floors by means of windows was one of yours. But perhaps that is only one of the talents necessary for your predilections." He frowned at his cravat in the mirror. "Let us lay that aside for now. What are we to do to help Reverend Durham? You can't mean to call on Lord Pergrine now?"

"But I must. It is very important, but not easily done." Dunstan frowned, shaking his head. With a shrug the mood was gone but not before Lin caught it. "Come now," the earl strove to lighten the atmosphere, "I am famished. Let us go to breakfast, my lord." He bowed and laughed at the grimace Lin tossed him in reply.

Sarita, driven to distraction with worry over the unexpected end of the militia meeting, her father's dark mood, and his refusal to answer any questions, along with the dowagers' maneuverings, was not surprised to find herself placed inextricably near "the earl" as the group began their walk to Mandel's. Her sister's scowling demeanour added to her difficulty. Matters worsened as the walk progressed, for not only was Sarita unsuccessful in her conversation attempts with "Lord Dunstan," who seemed oddly ill at ease, but Lady Imogene was keeping "Mr. Sullivan" and Deborah at the rear of the entourage with the baroness and Lady Phillippa in between.

It soon became apparent that only his lordship's secretary and Lady Imogene were conversing at all. Deborah refused to even look at Cris, and Lin was acting as if Sarita had contracted the plague.

With sighs of relief from everyone they arrived at Monsieur Mandel's greenhouses. At variance with the invitation, however, they found the doors firmly locked.

"I don't understand." Sarita rattled the handle once more. "Monsieur Mandel is seldom away from his work. He would never be gone after having invited us. I do hope nothing has happened to him. He has been so troubled and preoccupied of late."

"Do you think something is bothering him unduly?" Dunstan asked, his hand lightly touching hers as he reached to try the door.

"Yes, very much so." Sarita stumbled over the words, shocked by the strength of her reaction to his touch. "Perhaps we should force the door?" Her thoughts returned to Monsieur Mandel and the troubles in the area.

"That shall not be *nécessaire*." Pierre Mandel's voice came from one side of the greenhouse as he sauntered around the corner and came towards them. "My father wishes me to extend his *apologie*. Lord Pergrine has summoned him to the house." He shrugged, giving no further explanation.

"Could you not open the doors for us, Monsieur Mandel?" Lady Brienne asked.

A tight smile came to Pierre's lips. "It is my father's wish that he alone unveil his secret project to you." His smile broadened as he bowed. "But, come, let me walk with you as you return to the rectory. I should not like to be deprived of the opportunity to visit with you." He bowed to the women.

"Of course you may, Monsieur Mandel," Lady Imogene smiled.

"It is Pierre to you, madame," Mandel corrected her with a flourish.

"As you wish. We shall enjoy your company," Lady Phillippa agreed. "Sarita, you must walk with Monsieur Mandel." She edged the young woman forward, having decided that the earl needed a lesson in the effects of jealousy.

Bemoaning a second unsuitable companion, Sarita was cheered by a glance at Deborah, who at least had a chance to assume a place beside the "earl." With her sister appeased, she was certain the atmosphere would warm, and she stepped reluctantly towards young Mandel.

Neither young woman, however, had reckoned with the marchioness's skill at maneuvering them out of position. As the little band ambled back towards the rectory, Pierre and Sarita led, followed by Lin and Lady Brienne. Lady Imogene and the marchioness came next, and unchaperoned at the rear were Dunstan and Deborah, with neither wishing to take advantage of the opportunity arranged for them.

About half the distance had been covered when young Mandel halted abruptly, causing Lin to walk into him.

"Excuse me, sir," Lin apologized awkwardly.

"What is it, Pierre?" Sarita asked, growing concerned as his searching eyes swept across the area.

"I thought I heard a strange sound. Lord Pergrine has been increasingly plagued by poachers."

"But they have no reason to bother us," Lady Brienne said from behind them. "Let us go on."

Pierre shrugged, walked a few steps forward, and halted again. "My lord," he turned to Lin, "let us look about. I wish the *mesdames et mesdemoiselles* safe."

"If you insist," Lin replied reluctantly, looking askance as he thought of his highly polished pumps, his immaculate attire, and the heavy brush all about them.

"You shall look this way, and I the other," Pierre suggested and disappeared into the undergrowth.

"Shall I do it for you, my lord?" Dunstan asked lightly from the rear, his voice not betraying his sudden apprehension.

"No. It shall take but a few minutes," Lin answered and eased off the path. He had gone only a few paces when a shot sounded, followed closely by a second, and he fell to the ground.

Deborah screamed and took a hampering hold upon Cris, preventing him from rushing forward with Lady Brienne and Sarita. The countess and Lady Phillippa had crouched down at the sound of the gun blast but rose quickly and detached Miss Durham from the earl, who then vaulted into the brush.

Kneeling beside Lin, Sarita and the baroness managed to turn him over. Blood was seeping through his coat on the left side of his chest.

"Cloth. We must have cloth," Lady Brienne commanded. "Your petticoats, child," she waved impatiently.

The words finally taking on meaning, Sarita began ripping the flounce from her top petticoat.

Without noticeable success, Lady Phillippa and the countess tried to calm Deborah. "He is dead! Oh, he is dead. I know it," she screamed. When the baroness lifted his jacket and revealed even more blood, the distressed miss fell into a dead faint.

"Thank goodness," the countess said gratefully.

"Really, Imogene," Lady Phillippa reprimanded her sharply as she eased the young woman to the ground.

"Well, she would have convinced Lord Enoch he was near death if he became conscious," the lady defended herself and offered her reticule as a pillow.

"How is he, Brienne?" the marchioness questioned.

"It shall take a surgeon to remove the ball, but I am hopeful he shall recover. Actually Lord Enoch is quite fortunate. An inch or two lower and he would have no chance of survival," she answered, pressing the folds of the petticoat tightly to the wound.

Sounds of thrashing underbrush, snapping twigs, and fist slamming against flesh tightened a band of fear about the women. Sudden silence drew them, shivering, together.

Pierre Mandel broke through the undergrowth at the same instant that the earl pushed a bruised Clem Traunt into view.

"Clem!" Sarita rose in surprise and stepped towards him. "What has happened? Who has done this?"

"*Oui*, what has happened?" Pierre exclaimed. "I heard the shots and rushed back. *Mon Dieu!* Why, he has shot Lord Dunstan!" He stared at Clem.

"My thought exactly." The earl's voice was cold and hard as he pushed against the arm he had wrenched behind Traunt's back and raised a fowling piece in his free hand for all to see.

"But Clem would never have shot Lord Dunstan," Sarita protested angrily, striding forward and attempting to take Cris's hold from him.

112

"Here is the gun, newly fired," Dunstan clipped, refusing to release him.

"Let us all regain our senses," Lady Brienne snapped. "Would you prefer that Enoch bleed to death while you haggle? Mr. Traunt will not seek to escape. We must get his lordship to the rectory and summon a surgeon to attend him," she ordered.

Dunstan dropped his hold; his eyes flickered to Sarita as she ripped a further piece of cloth from her petticoat and used it to stay the blood from Traunt's lower lip. Concern for his cousin overrode all else and he knelt down at Lin's side.

"I could go at once for Dr. Simpson," Pierre offered. "He attends Lord Pergrine and other gentry in this area."

"Be gone then," the baroness barked. "Mr. Sullivan, you and Mr. Traunt can carry Enoch to the rectory."

"Let me see the wound," Dunstan commanded, and the baroness raised the blood-soaked compress and watched as he probed expertly.

"You are familiar with wounds of this sort, Mr. Sullivan?" asked the baroness.

"I served briefly in the army," he returned, giving her a sharp look. "Can we have a fresh compress?" His eyes swung to Sarita.

"Of course," she replied and hurriedly tore a flounce from her second petticoat.

Dunstan took it and pressed it in place. Speaking curtly, he instructed the baroness, "Keep it tightly held. Traunt, take his feet. Carefully now."

From Lin Sullivan's forbidding, worry-riden features to her sister's pale face as she lay upon the ground, Sarita looked at Lord Enoch's ashen colour in a daze. The fear and tension of the last few weeks had exploded far too close.

Chapter XI

"Where is that surgeon?" Dunstan asked impatiently as he came from the bedchamber.

"Pierre will have him here soon," Sarita reassured him. "Here are the towels Lady Brienne asked for. How is Lord Dunstan?"

"Losing far too much blood. The surgeon should have been here by now." Anger edged his voice.

"He will come soon." Sarita laid a hand on the man's arm to comfort him. The anguish on his face wrenched her. "Do you fear he shall die?"

"It is possible."

"We are all to die," she said gently.

"But he would not be there but for I."

"Sarita! Sarita!" Lady Phillippa came running up the stairs. "Dr. Simpson has arrived."

"Send him up at once," Dunstan called to her. Taking the towels from Sarita, he returned to the bedchamber.

The tasty, cold roast set upon the table as an early supper was hardly being touched. Mrs. Durham, her composure more ruffled than usual by the circumstances, sat picking at the lace on her kerchief as the others stared wordlessly at their plates. "Should we not eat?" she asked nervously. "Food must never be wasted. Oh, it is so late. Where can John be? Oh, dear, what shall we do?" Lines of uncertainty and confusion clearly etched her face.

"Oh, Mother, I don't see why you insisted we serve this," Deborah snapped. "No one has eaten a bite."

Sarita motioned to her sister to be silent.

"How can you speak to me in that way?" Mrs. Durham burst into tears.

"Mother, must you always . . ."

"Let me take you to your chamber," Lady Phillippa interrupted Deborah's words, rising from her chair and going to Mrs. Durham's side.

Smiling her thanks, Sarita also rose and clamped a hand on her sister's shoulder. "No more," she whispered sternly.

"Let us put the food away." Lady Imogene pushed back from the table. "Even I find no taste for anything this eve."

"I have the cure for that," the earl said as he entered the room smiling.

"Lord Dunstan?" the women asked as one.

"Will happily recover, completely. The ball has been removed and the bleeding halted."

"Thank the lord." Lady Phillippa spoke for them all.

"Lady Brienne asked that you come to the earl's bedchamber," he told Sarita.

"I'll go at once," she answered, approaching him. "I am so glad," she said softly, pausing before him, then hurried from his searching look.

"Let us eat," Dunstan told the women with an exaggerated wave at the table. "Mrs. Durham"—he spoke gently as she and the marchioness moved forward—"surely you mean to partake of this delicious

116

food. May I not seat you?" His calm voice assured and steadied her, and she allowed him to return her to her chair.

"Sarita! Sarita," Reverend Durham's voice reached the dining salon.

"She has gone upstairs," Lord Dunstan explained, going into the corridor.

"I just heard the news. How does the earl fare?" the rector asked, his face haggard.

"He will recover, with little but the scar to tell of his wound," Dunstan told him. "We were just about to savour a cold collation." He motioned to the dining salon.

"My wife . . . ?"

"Mrs. Durham was naturally . . . upset over the . . . incident, but she is calm now. Your presence would perhaps be steadying." He studied Durham closely as he spoke.

The rector sighed. "Yes, I suppose so. I had not meant to be so long, but after this morn's . . ." His words ended vaguely. "Do tell me what happened," he said, signing for the secretary to return to the dining salon ahead of him. The episode was quickly told.

"We saw no one," Lady Imogene answered when questioned by Reverend Durham, "until Monsieur Mandel and Mr. Sullivan appeared with Mr. Traunt in tow." She paused, perplexed. "I wonder where Monsieur Mandel could be now? He left immediately after coming with Dr. Simpson."

"Why is he not here?" Dunstan echoed the question. "Where is Traunt?"

"Mr. Traunt is in the kitchen," Lady Phillippa

117

said. "He left briefly to attend to something on his farm but has returned."

"I cannot believe Clem Traunt is responsible for this." Reverend Durham's deep voice held a firm conviction. "He has been steadfast in supporting my actions and has no need to poach. Besides, his marksmanship is excellent. He would never have taken Lord Dunstan for a partridge. Have you heard his account of what happened?"

Dunstan grimaced painfully. "No, my concern was for my cousin."

"Quite understandable, Mr. Sullivan, but matters are calmer now," Durham noted. "Deborah, ask Mr. Traunt to join us."

Petulantly, the young woman rose and did as bid. She returned quickly. In fresh attire and with his cuts and bruises tended, Mr. Traunt followed.

"Reverend Durham, don't be believing what he says," Clem waved at Dunstan.

"I asked you to come and tell us what you saw, Clem," the rector reassured him.

Red tinged Traunt's cheeks under Dunstan's gaze, and with a mixture of anger and embarrassment in his voice he said, "I was on my way to the rectory, to call on Miss Sarita." He looked up from the hat in his hands challengingly. "You know I seldom use the path, Reverend."

A nod assured him.

"Well, I heard these voices and realized it was the ladies." Traunt nodded at the dowagers. "I was makin' to join them when I saw a man takin' aim at somethin'. He didn't look like no one from here, so I went his way to see what mischief he was up to.

118

When I was still several paces away from the bloke, he fires and I realizes it was at them ladies he shot. He took off a-runnin', but I got off a shot. Hit him too. Would have had him if it weren't for that one." His look condemned the earl as he tenderly touched a bruise on his jaw. "Right good he is with his hands, but cause o' him the guilty bloke got clear away. Followed his trail this afternoon, but it ended." Traunt's eyes swung back to the rector.

"What direction did he take?" the earl asked.

"Round about at first, it was. First towards Pergrine's, then back towards them plant houses of the Frenchman, Mandel." Clem met his gaze steadily.

"I regret my hasty actions, Mr. Traunt," Dunstan and, rising and walking around the table. "I hope you understand they were caused by my concern for my cousin." He extended his hand in apology.

"Likely'd done the same," Clem muttered, accepting the hand. "Would feel better if I'd a landed at least one blow."

"In justice, you deserve the opportunity," Dunstan smiled. "Whenever you choose . . ."

"Don't say I care to." Clem attempted a smile with his swollen lip.

"Then come, both of you, sit down," Durham invited. "Partake of this delicious fare the ladies have served."

After a second handshake, the men turned to the table. Everyone but Reverend Durham fell enthusiastically upon the cold beef, roast hen, biscuits, breads, and spiced fruits which lay before them.

Lady Brienne returned to her bedchamber in mid-eve to find her sisters awaiting her. "You should be abed," she scolded them. "How are you to take your turn sitting with Lord Enoch if you do not rest?"

"We had to speak with you, Brienne." Lady Imogene shook her head at the baroness's tone.

"How is Enoch?" Lady Phillippa asked.

"Sleeping quietly. He seems calmer with Sarita's handling. I feel I have aged twenty years this day." She sat down and passed a hand across her eyes.

"But don't you see, Brienne, even this unfortunate occurrence has hidden blessings," Lady Phillippa told her happily. "With Sarita caring for Enoch, their match is a certainty."

"Our nephew is in no condition to compromise Miss Durham," Lady Brienne returned caustically.

"This time of trouble will bring them closer," the countess countered seriously. "Philly means he will be grateful to Sarita and . . ."

"Gratitude does not a marriage make," the baroness refused to agree.

"Oh, Brienne, you . . ." Lady Imogene spluttered.

A wave of the baroness's hand silenced her. "I am far too fatigued for this." She shook her head. "Instead of pursuing your matchmaking, you should be searching for reasons why Enoch was shot. Death was the intent."

Gasps came from both sisters. "You cannot be serious," they said in unison.

"Am I in this room?" she returned acidly. "We shall call on Monsieur Mandel, both Messieurs Mandel, at the first opportunity. My bones tell me the answer lies in their direction."

"But why? Pierre only met Enoch on the eve past and his father never has," Lady Phillippa protested.

"You had as lief accuse Lord Pergrine," the countess snorted.

"Perhaps I shall," Lady Brienne returned coldly. "Perhaps I shall."

The tread of steps too heavy for a woman's and yet not her father's warned Sarita of Mr. Sullivan's approach as she sat at Lord Dunstan's side.

Entering, Cris paused and studied her features, the glow of the bedside lamp giving them a warm, bewitching glow. The earl moaned and she took his hand. For the first time in his life Cris felt a twinge of envy.

"I see he sleeps easily," he whispered.

Still holding the earl's hand, Sarita nodded. "The dowagers are to take turns keeping watch through the night," she spoke softly. "You may feel at ease about his lordship and retire yourself." She gave him a heartwarming smile.

"I must go out—a matter of importance to the earl that needs attention," Dunstan returned without thinking, his eyes moving to his cousin's ashen face.

"It is far too late for any business matter," she challenged, her voice rising above a whisper.

The earl put a finger to his lips. "You are, perhaps, correct," he amended his error. "Yes, I shall retire." He searched her features as concern diminished in them. "Good eve. Thank you for caring for my cousin. It shall not go unrewarded."

"I seek nothing," Sarita blushed. "It is but a duty, gladly done."

"And you are keenly tied to duty," Dunstan returned softly with sudden intuition.

Sarita stared at him questioningly. "Should it not be so?"

He bowed, his curious expression troubling her, then went to the small bedchamber and closed the door behind him.

What could he have meant? the young woman asked herself. *And why does his mere look disquiet me so?*

A crescent moon hung in the sky as Lord Dunstan gingerly worked his way along the stone ledge outside the window to the trellis and down the wall. Dropping to the ground, he crouched, awaiting any sign that he had been detected. None came, and he quickly slipped past the garden. Hurried steps took him deep into the woods and, by a prearranged plan, he found a saddled mount awaiting him. The dense forest muffled the steed's steps as they made their way to the main road. Once on it, Dunstan set his spurs into his mount's flanks. The gelding, fresh and long-limbed, ran smoothly and quickly. In good time Dunstan reined to a halt outside the small village of Runnet, not far from Hastings.

Three times the earl gave an owl's hoot, pausing after each reply. A signal came on the last call. Easing his mount forward, he pulled a pistol from his waistband, cradling it gently in his hand.

A tall, thin man stepped forward slowly from behind a huge boulder. He stopped at hearing the pistol being cocked. "No need fer that," he spoke hurriedly. "It be Billy."

"Alone?"

"Aye, like I were told."

"Do you have anything for me?" Dunstan still held the pistol loosely pointed in the man's direction.

"This." Billy held up a pouch. "If ye can prove ye be Henry Edward." His coastal twang had been dropped. "And how am I to know you are he?" He lowered the pouch.

"*Caeteris paribus*," Dunstan returned, lowering his pistol. "Other things being equal."

"*Bonus*," Billy returned and approached the earl as he dismounted. "I dare not stay long. All we have learned is in this." He handed over the pouch. "Have you a message in return?"

"Tell them Lord Dunstan has been wounded but will recover."

"Lord Dunstan!" the other repeated in surprise.

"Just give the message. What have you learned in Hastings? Has the name Mandel come up?"

"So far only rumours about the usual smuggling. No one has spoken of a Mandel as far as I know, but there has been little time. When shall we meet next?"

"In a fortnight, unless you learn something important. Has Pergrine been mentioned?"

"Pergrine? It is odd you speak of him. I saw him just two days past. Overheard him talking with two sailors. He is a harmless-looking man," Billy shrugged.

"Did you hear what was said?" Dunstan asked impatiently.

"Something about a cargo. Didn't think we'd be interested. Probably more French brandy. Why this interest?"

"A feeling. Keep your ears keen on it. If you need to contact me, there is a bog on the secondary road between here and Pordean. A large limb now lies on the east side of it. Move that limb to the west side, and I will meet you at the bog on the next night. Be wary; I fear we may be watched."

The thin man nodded assent. "Jervy's here. Says to tell you he'll be handy if you need him," Billy said lowly. "A safe return," he added and disappeared into the darkness.

Dunstan mounted and turned back towards Braitlathe. The attempt on Lin's life had made this a personal matter, one to be resolved quickly. His mind raced through the dabs of information he had. He prayed that the pouch contained something helpful.

Chapter XII

"Deborah—Miss Durham—and I have concurred," Lord Dunstan said, entering Lin's bedchamber, "that today you shall have an outing."

"But Dr. Simpson said I was to remain abed two days more," his cousin threw back plaintively.

"Not you, my lord. Sarita—Miss Durham—is to have the outing," the earl corrected himself archly, gazing at the wan girl seated beside the bed with an open book on her lap.

"And I will care for you, my lord," Deborah added, looking around the earl's broad shoulders.

"But Lady Brienne . . . oh." Sarita threw aside all guilt. "I am certain Deborah will attend you very well," she assured Lin, giving the coverlet a straightening tap. "His lordship needs to remain quiet," she said, turning to her sister. "Perhaps you could read to him, Deborah," she suggested.

"We shall manage very well," her sister answered, taking her hand and leading her towards the door. "You enjoy your walk with Mr. Sullivan."

"Unless you prefer to sit in the garden," Cris said, his eyes teasing.

"A walk will do very well," Sarita said before Deborah pushed her through the doorway.

With a wink at Lin and a low bow for the eager young woman at his cousin's bedside, Dunstan sauntered into the corridor and found Sarita gone. "Could it be the lady disliked my interference?" he murmured. "Where could she have gone?" Snapping his fingers as an idea blossomed, he hurried down the stairs, ran through the Hall and out the front doors. "Just what I thought," he allowed, seeing Sarita on the path to Mandel's. "Miss Durham," he called after her, his hurried stride drawing him near her quickly.

Glancing back, Sarita flashed him a challenging smile, gathered up her skirts, and took off running. Two weeks of being confined for most of the day with Lord Dunstan had often made her want to bolt, and she did so now.

"A race it is," Dunstan shouted, laughing.

Sarita ran nimbly, easily hopping over small branches on the path, but Dunstan slowly gained on her. Seeing he was almost upon her, she sprinted forward, but in her hurry, a corner of her petticoat slipped from her hand.

When he saw this and realized she was headed for a tumble, Dunstan leaped forward and grabbed her about the waist, swinging her off her feet.

The sudden stop was a surprise, but finding herself cradled in Mr. Sullivan's powerful arms, his laughing eyes and smiling face so close, silenced her protests. For a long moment they gazed at one another. The laughter slowly left the earl's eyes, replaced by something Sarita refused to read. Spellbound, his lips were about to close on hers when she awakened from her trancelike state, drawing back in alarm. "Mr. Sullivan," she protested breathlessly.

"I only wished to keep you from tripping." He

forced a bantering tone and reluctantly set her upon the ground.

"That was . . . well, thank you." She straightened her skirts, keeping her eyes lowered, her emotions in a welter of confusion as she realized that she wished to be still in his arms.

"It is not oft I find a near match to my speed," he laughed lightly. "Especially among a member of your fair gender." Dunstan bowed with a slight flourish.

Red flared to Sarita's cheeks as she misread the gesture. "Perhaps you should turn around at once and inform the dowagers that their selection of a nurse-maid for the earl is far too unladylike for his lord-ship's sensibilities. I am certain he would agree," she said hotly, her dark eyes flashing in anger.

"I would gladly do as you suggest if it were true, for it would free you." His strange look held Sarita fast. "It is not easy to visit with one who is attending a wounded man," Dunstan explained.

"Visit . . . ? You should have to care for one such as Lord Dunstan. The last two weeks have been . . ." she blurted, halting with a true blush on her fine features. "I . . . I apologize. Though you do not know what it is to care for his lordship," she said weakly, then added hastily, "no one is in good form when not well."

"His lordship a trying man? I cannot see it," Dun-stan said in a highly serious tone, a mischievous glint in his eye betraying him.

Reading the tease, Sarita threw her hands in the air and burst into laughter. "I don't know which of you is more trying," she gasped, drawing a deep breath. "No, Deborah has drawn the harder lot, I dare say. I don't know how you tolerate his lordship's constant fussiness. Oh, pardon me again. I fear my words are too quick." She looked at him apologetically.

"Oh, I agree with you completely," he smiled, offering his arm. "Shall we continue . . . at a walk?"

Sarita laid her hand lightly on his arm, her heart lurching tremulously as he laid his own over hers. "We . . . we had better go on," she said softly.

With a smile, Dunstan removed his hand and stepped forward. They walked silently, deep in thought until Mandel's greenhouses appeared before them.

Halting, Sarita removed her hand from his arm. "I would like to see Monsieur Mandel alone," she said, a hint of reluctance in her tone and regret creasing her smile.

"Pierre Mandel?" Dunstan asked, more than half serious.

"Pierre? Never. What can you be thinking? I promised Monsieur Mandel . . ."

"Ah, his secret project," the earl said, recalling the younger Frenchman's words.

"Yes," she said with obvious relief. "It is very important to him."

"Then I shall await you here."

"Oh, no. . . . I know how busy you have been . . ." Sarita paused as he cocked an eyebrow. "Lady Imogene tells me what transpires during the day when she comes to relieve me in the evening. Who has come and gone and such," she explained, her colour rising beneath his smiling, knowing eyes.

"I do not like to think of you returning to the rectory unescorted," he said, looking thoughtful.

"But I have always gone about alone. There is no one who would harm me."

"Perhaps not, but I prefer to be assured of your safety," Dunstan insisted lightly.

"I will be here for a very uncertain length of time. But perhaps I have a solution. Today is Tuesday, is it not? Clem, Mr. Traunt, delivers a cart of manure on Tuesday of each week for Monsieur Mandel's gardens. He shall be happy to walk me home," Sarita ended. Pleased that she had kept him from the inconvenience of waiting for her, she was perplexed by the hint of questioning reluctance she saw. "You cannot think Clem had anything to do with Lord Dunstan's . . ."

"No. As you wish it to be." The earl bowed slightly. "May Monsieur Mandel's project prosper," he added with a smile.

"Why, thank you, Mr. Sullivan. Till this eve."

"Assuredly."

Sarita walked a few paces, then turned back to him. "Thank you . . . for rescuing me from the sickroom. I believe Lord Dunstan and I would have come to blows had we been forced to go on together, except that he is too much a gentleman for that," she added.

"Till this eve." Dunstan tipped his hat and watched her petite figure lithely run to the greenhouse. At the door she waved to him. Dunstan chuckled to himself. The more he thought about what Sarita had said, the higher his spirits rose, and he whistled gaily as with quick strides he returned to the rectory.

"Why, Mr. Sullivan, how cheerful you sound," Lady Phillippa greeted Dunstan as he entered the Hall.

"And how lovely you are today." He bowed.

"Flattery. Excellent." Her eyes twinkled merrily. "But someone in your questionable position needs such a grace."

"Now what could I have done?" Dunstan asked grinning.

"I almost think you are Irish, Mr. Sullivan, the blarney rolls so easily off your tongue." The marchioness studied him with folded hands. "But Sarita did need an outing, I suppose. Though I must admit I had hoped to see more interest between the two."

"Do I detect a hint o' the matchmaker in ye?" he teased in an Irish brogue.

"By sure and by golly," she countered in like tones. "What better way to cement a relationship than nursing. Why, Enoch will be much easier to deal with once he is wed. You will see."

"That could be."

"And Sarita is just the wife for him." Lady Phillippa's eyes grew dreamy. "What a lovely countess she will make."

"That I must agree with," Dunstan said with a wink and sauntered off, leaving the marchioness with the oddest feeling that he was thoroughly enjoying a jest.

"I must go now, *monsieur*. I promised Mr. Sullivan that Clem would walk me home. Some foolishness

130

about my safety," Sarita explained as she took off her work apron and hung it up.

"A wise young man, that one," Mandel noted.

"You know Mr. Sullivan?"

"He has visited me once or twice since that unfortunate *affaire* with Lord Dunstan. Beneath all his jesting there is a knowledgeable young man."

Sarita smiled with pleasure as she nodded her agreement.

"Are you ready, Miss Sarita?" Clem stuck his head through the entrance. "Unloaded as usual, Mr. Mandel."

"*Merci*, Monsieur Traunt. Remember, *mademoiselle*, this eve."

"I could not forget, *monsieur*," Sarita assured him. "I have not been able to help you as much as I wished and am glad for this opportunity."

"There will be no problem about your coming?"

"I will manage it," Sarita smiled. "Good day."

"Hurry, Sarita," Clem called. "I must return to the farm quickly. My best cow is about to calve."

"Till this eve." She waved at the old Frenchman and hurried out.

"An odd man, Mr. Sullivan," Mandel murmured, watching Sarita go, "to wish her escorted by another."

"I can go on alone, Clem, if you think it best you return now," she told the long-stepping, burly young farmer as she half ran to catch up with him.

"No, Sullivan is right. No one is safe until we learn who is behind the murders. I'll walk with you to the edge of the woods. You should be safe enough once in the open," Traunt said brusquely, slowing his steps.

"What do you think of Mr. Sullivan, Clem?" Sarita asked, still running every third step to keep apace.

"He's a smart enough sort. Don't strike me as a secretary or whatever he says he is," Clem snorted.

"But he's been so busy seeing to the earl's affairs."

"Here you be. Hurry to the rectory now." Traunt halted at the edge of the woods.

"But . . . Thank you, Clem." She raised her skirts and ran across the meadow, his statement about Mr. Sullivan troubling her.

It was near ten in the evening when Sarita and Deborah retired to their bedchamber.

"Father seemed grim this eve . . . more so than usual," Sarita noted as she sat at her dressing table brushing her long black hair. "I wish he would confide in someone. What do you think, Debs?" She turned to her sister, who was dreamily pulling on her nightdress. "Debs?"

"What were you saying?"

"Didn't you notice Father at supper? He hardly spoke a word," Sarita repeated, surprised that her sister had not noticed.

"Was something wrong? I saw nothing unusual." Deborah blinked innocently.

"I don't think you have seen anything since you left Lord Dunstan's chamber," the elder snorted.

"Lord Enoch," Deborah sighed, hearing nothing but the name. "Such a gentleman. One would think it would be very uncomfortable being alone with a gentleman, but he was so . . . kind. And he bears his wound so bravely."

"Did she sit with the same man?" Sarita muttered to herself.

"Do you think I could sit with Lord Enoch again on the morrow?" Deborah pleaded.

"Nothing would please me more, but Lady Phillippa. . . ?"

"Just tell the marchioness that you do not care for Lord Enoch. You don't, do you?" she asked fearfully.

"Heaven forbid it."

"How can you say that?" Deborah challenged contrarily.

"Do you want me to care for him?"

"No, but the ladies do. I overheard Lady Phillippa tell Mr. Sullivan what a perfect countess you would make."

"She didn't," Sarita gasped.

"I don't see why you are upset. They want you to wed his lordship." She flounced angrily upon her bed. "I suppose all you care about is that Mr. Sullivan you've been mooning over."

"I have not."

"An ordinary secretary," the younger taunted.

"What matter a man's station in life if he is doing the best he can," Sarita countered. "If you truly loved Lord Dunstan you wouldn't care what he was, earl or not."

Deborah shrugged and pulled back the bedcovers, climbing in. "I don't care if you prefer Mr. Sullivan, Sarry, even though he is a secretary, for Lord Enoch is an earl," she ended archly and turned her back.

Grimacing at her, Sarita rose, laying down her hairbrush. Blowing out the lamp by her bed, she lay down and waited. Soon Deborah's breathing sounded slow and easy, bespeaking sleep. Silently, Sarita rose, pulled her long-sleeved dressing gown over her nightdress and stole from the bedchamber. Feeling her way in the dark, she found the stairs and stole down to the kitchen. There she pulled a carriage lamp she had hidden earlier from beneath the cupboard and lit it. Dressing quickly with the garments she had also placed there, she soon hurried out the back door and across the meadow.

Upstairs, the earl was gazing out the east windows as he endured the third repetition of Lin's praises for the younger Miss Durham. A flicker of light caught his eye. "I am certain Miss Durham is as charming as you say, Lin," he cut him off, turning to face the bed. "But you should be asleep. Even I feel fatigued. Good eve."

Lin watched open-mouthed as the earl strode across the chamber to the connecting room and shut the door.

"There, the work is done." Mandel surveyed the plants they had been working with. "It is silly, I suppose, to be so careful, but this is *très important* to me. *Merci!*"

"I didn't mind, *monsieur*," Sarita told him sincerely. "I regret not having been able to help you these past weeks, but I must go now, before I am missed. Mother sometimes awakens."

"*Oui*, I shall walk with you."

"I would appreciate that. All this talk of danger has begun to make me hear things. You know, I even thought I was being followed when I came." Sarita laughed lightly.

Monsieur Mandel went to his desk and removed a small pistol. "Only for assurance," he told her. Lighting the carriage lamp, he guided her from the greenhouse, halting when they reached the meadow's edge.

Watching from a distance, Dunstan saw them speak briefly, then part. He shadowed Sarita until she entered the kitchen door, then headed back through the woods for a rendezvous of his own.

Trust her, his heart overrode his mind's suspicions. *Trust her.*

Chapter XIII

"Be careful, Father. Slowly now." Deborah hovered nervously at the bottom of the steps as Reverend Durham assisted Lin down the broad stairs.

"Lean on me, my lord," she told him when they reached the bottom. "We have a chair especially prepared for you in the garden."

"I believe I can manage it, sir," Lin told the rector as Deborah took hold of his right arm. "My strength has quite returned in the past two days. Lady Brienne was perfectly correct in thinking that walking in my chamber would aid my recovery."

"But you must not overdo," Deborah warned, her eyes brightening as a result of his smile.

"Then I shall let you children go on," Reverend Durham told the pair. "I shall be in my study if you require assistance." Suppressing a chuckle when the two showed no sign of having heard him, he turned and walked away.

The sound of his footsteps broke the spell between the pair. "Father, where will you be if Lord Dunstan needs help coming in?" Deborah asked.

"In the study . . . the library. You had best go on. I believe everyone awaits you."

"Yes, Mother and the dowagers have prepared a special tea to mark your coming from the sickroom," Deborah told Lin as they walked slowly towards the front doors. "How pleasant it will be to have you join us once again."

"I rather . . . regret . . . the change," Lin said, halting and gazing steadily at her. "The past few days that you have sat with me have been . . ." He colored slightly. "I have . . ." Words failed to come.

A sudden shyness struck Deborah as she realized his intent. "I, too, have found them . . . enjoyable," she murmured.

"We mustn't keep the ladies and your mother waiting," Lin managed, and the pair continued through the hall.

Outdoors, the dowagers and Mrs. Durham awaited Lord Enoch, their tea and cakes in readiness. A chair with cushions had been placed in the arbour for his lordship, but he bravely disdained its use, insisting he felt truly recovered.

"Were you not to be weeding the garden?" Lady Imogene asked Deborah, outmaneuvering her from sitting beside Lin.

"Sarita said she did not mind doing it," Deborah responded with a hint of a pout.

"She is far more content out of doors than Deborah," Mrs. Durham said.

"She did want to do it," Deborah added defensively.

"Very well, child. I meant nothing by the question." The countess gave her hand a pat. "Here is your tea. Try one of these cakes," she said, offering the platter of prettily decorated sweets.

"Your tea is excellent, Mrs. Durham, and I can only give the highest praise to you for your cakes, Lady

Imogene," Lin told the ladies sometime later. "This has been most pleasant. But now I would like to walk about a bit. Try my legs, so to speak." He smiled, much of his former nervousness gone after such close contact with the women during his nursing.

"I shall go with you, Lord Dunstan," Deborah said, standing. "There is a rather delightful brook . . ."

"We would all like to see it, would we not?" Lady Phillippa rose.

"But, my ladies, I would not wish you to strain yourselves," Lin protested.

"Then Mrs. Durham and I shall remain behind," Lady Brienne told him. "Someone must clear away the tea. If you see Josh or Ben, send them to me."

"As you wish," Sullivan acceded with a bow.

"May I take your arm?" Lady Phillippa asked, taking hold. "Deborah, you must walk before us to show the way."

"Yes, my lady," she answered, forgetting to pout for the warmth of Lin's smile.

The baroness had observed the pair closely as Deborah reluctantly took the lead. The action and reactions between the young man and woman during tea had confirmed her growing suspicions. A council would have to be held, for it was plain her sisters were still blind to the obvious.

"I suppose your mother never speaks of us," Lady Phillippa broached the tender subject.

"M-my mother?" Lin's nervousness returned. He began fidgeting with his cravat. "No, I don't believe she does," he managed through a large gulp.

"How is her health?"

"She is . . . well. I saw her before I left London to come here, and she was very well," the earl's cousin said with slightly more assurance.

"Did she object to your coming to see us?" the countess asked, having come to Lin's other side.

"Lady Dunstan—Mother—would never do that, would she? I mean you are her sisters . . ."

Wonderment at that unusual reply lasted only a fraction of a second as a shot rang out, the ball leaving a tear in Lin's left jacket sleeve.

At sight of the rip, Lady Imogene pushed against him with all her weight, sending them both sprawling and bringing the marchioness down beneath them.

Seeing Dunstan fall, Deborah broke into a deafening shriek and fainted.

The sound of the shot had startled Sarita, and her sister's scream propelled her from the garden at a dead run. Reaching the front of the house, she paused momentarily, searching. The baroness, who had come to the front door, pointed towards the group in the meadow, all four on the grass. Flashes of petticoats and excited chatter told them that the dowagers were unharmed. The sight of Lin trying to free himself from them confirmed his condition. Only Deborah's plight remained uncertain. Dashing to the group, Sarita panted, "What has happened?" and helped Lady Phillippa up while Lin, finally freed, assisted the countess.

"Has Deborah been shot?" She looked at her sister.

"Someone tried to shoot Enoch. See." The countess grabbed hold of the torn sleeve.

"Deborah!" came from Lin's lips as he saw her prone figure. "She's been shot." He blanched white.

139

"She has only fainted, Enoch." The marchioness looked up as she knelt beside Sarita at the young woman's side. "See, she is coming to her senses."

The light brown lashes fluttered as he dropped to one knee at her side and took one of her hands in his. Her eyes met his concerned gaze as they opened. "Enoch," she breathed.

"You are unhurt?"

"And you?" Deborah asked, nodding.

"Only my sleeve needs mending," Lin assured her.

"Let me help you rise, Deborah." The countess bent over and took hold of her elbow. Lady Phillippa took the other.

"Do you really think someone is . . . is attempting to murder you?" Sarita asked Lin. "Oh, where is Mr. Sullivan? He has been gone so much of late."

"Cris has many business matters to attend to . . . for me of course—especially since I have been disabled." Lin's eyes shifted back to Deborah. "Let us hasten indoors. Miss Durham looks far from well."

"How fortunate I find you here," Pierre Mandel greeted Sarita later that same afternoon as she came from the garden, supper's carrots cradled in her apron. "Is it true another attempt was made on Lord Dunstan's life?"

"I fear so, although Lord Enoch insists that no one wishes him harm," Sarita replied, continuing towards the kitchen door, wishing it was much closer.

"*Certainement,* he must jest," Mandel said in surprise.

"Why do you say that?" she asked, halting.

"Not only are there many husbands seeking to

140

reckon with him, but there is Monsieur Sullivan," Pierre told her matter-of-factly.

"Mr. Sullivan? You cannot be serious," she laughed. "No one is more concerned for Lord Enoch's safety."

"*Oui?* And where was he today?"

"Attending to business. Lord Enoch himself told me," Sarita threw back.

"Does it not seem at odds with his regard for his lordship to be absent on Lord Enoch's first day from the sick chamber?"

"I am certain he felt there was no danger," she insisted, her ire growing at Pierre's persistence.

"Did you know Monsieur Sullivan is a cousin of the earl's?"

"Of course."

"And that he is next in line for the title?" Pierre arched an eyebrow meaningfully.

"How do you know this?" she demanded.

"I have friends among the peerage who know Lord Dunstan, and they believe Monsieur Sullivan covets his nervous cousin's wealth."

"I don't believe that."

"*Non?* You have been beguiled, like many others. Monsieur Sullivan's reputation as a womanizer is equal to that of his lordship's."

"That has nothing to do with this."

"But do you not recall how the man who shot Lord Dunstan escaped because of Monsieur Sullivan's interference?"

Sarita shook her head in disbelief.

"I shall say no more. I wish only to warn you. Think; does Monsieur Sullivan act the humble secretary? Take care, *mademoiselle*. Feel free to call on me. I will gladly aid you in any way."

"Thank you, Monsieur Mandel." Sarita met his gaze, then flitted her eyes away, fearful he might read in them the uneasiness his words had aroused. "Thank you. I must go," she ended curtly.

"*Adieu*," he called after her. "Ah, *monsieur*," he spoke softly to himself, "the seed is well planted." Chuckling, he sauntered on his way.

In the kitchen Sarita dumped her bundle of carrots into a basin and scrubbed them furiously. Pierre's words tumbled over one another in her mind. The slam of the front doors drew her from her thoughts. The first outburst was followed by a less violent, but loud, shutting of the library's door. Wiping her hands on her apron, Sarita hurried to the library and entered without knocking. She stopped short at the sight of her father downing a stiff glass of sherry.

"Father," she exclaimed, seeing his dusty, torn coat and bruised face. "What has happened?"

"Lord Pergrine tries Christian patience beyond endurance," the deep voice rumbled.

"He did this to you?"

"No, some of his hired bullies did." The rector sank into the chair behind his desk. I must think." He dropped his head into his hands.

"Please, Father." Sarita rushed to his side and dropped to her knees, reaching to draw his hands from his face. "Tell me what happened."

"Lord Pergrine's blackguards caught witless Tom Trumbull and his brother, Ned, poaching last night . . . or so they claim. I hurried over to Pergrine Manor as soon as I heard of it this morn. First, I was made to wait—for hours it seemed—and then I was finally allowed a few minutes alone with the two men. It was dreadful how they had been beaten. They told me Pergrine means to hang them."

"He can't."

"He can. A peer's lands are inviolable and he is the magistrate. When I left the two, I demanded to see Pergrine. He knows they are harmless halfwits. I pleaded to see him, but his men laughed. I lost my temper and stepped toward one. I fully intended to hit him, but this happened"—he pointed to the bruise on his jaw—"before I could do any harm."

"What will become of Tom and Ned?"

"They will be hanged in the morn unless something is done."

"Oh, what are we to do?"

"You are to do nothing, my precious little princess. After I change, I will go to see Clem Traunt. Mayhap he will be willing to . . ."

"But couldn't you all be imprisoned for attempting to free them?"

"Hush, daughter. Go fetch me a fresh shirt and coat. I don't care to have your mother see me thus. I will make for the kitchen and try to repair some of this damage." He tried to smile and grimaced painfully instead.

Both saw the earl as they turned to the door.

"The latter would be wise, Reverend Durham, but I strongly advise against your former intentions," Dunstan said, stepping into the library and closing the door behind him.

"Mr. Sullivan, you are unfamiliar with our problems," the rector returned carefully.

"But I do know the danger in which you would be placing yourself and anyone else who chose to follow you. Think of your wife . . . your family," Dunstan continued persuasively. "What would they do, deprived of your presence, of the livelihood you provide?"

Reverend Durham burst into laughter. Sarita stared at him, hesitant.

The earl looked at the pair in rueful surprise.

"Pardon me, Mr. Sullivan, but is it really unknown to you that we have no funds? Lord Dunstan has been providing for all since his arrival."

"He has?" Dunstan asked slowly. "Nevertheless, that does not alter my point."

"You have no point, Mr. Sullivan. Lord Pergrine would not harm me."

Dunstan waved at the rector's battered face.

His men did this," Reverend Durham said. "He would not have permitted it had he been present. I know the man better than you."

"Father must do something," Sarita said, stepping towards Dunstan. "Can you not see that?"

"There are more ways of helping them than by endangering others. What if Lord Dunstan were to speak with Lord Pergrine?"

"I do not believe that would alter anything." Durham shook his head.

"You must let us try," the earl insisted.

"Why do you take such an interest?" The rector studied the young man carefully.

"Do you intend to go ahead with your plan to rescue the men?" Dunstan asked coldly.

"Yes."

"Then I shall be forced to warn Pergrine."

"No!" Sarita gasped. "You wouldn't."

"If I must. Don't you see, Sarita, it is the only way to save your father, Clem, and any others foolish enough to attempt it." His eyes pleaded for her understanding.

"But he won't let you go," Sarita told him, on the brink of tears.

"Quiet, daughter. Mr. Sullivan is only doing as his conscience bids, and he should be respected for that. I will agree," he told him, "if you can convince Lord Dunstan to call upon Lord Pergrine this eve and persuade him to delay the proceedings."

"Good," Dunstan said readily. "Where is his lordship?"

"In the solarium," Sarita told him. Her large and accusingly damp eyes lurched his heart. "Someone attempted to shoot Lord Dunstan this afternoon," she told the men.

"What?" both asked, Dunstan blanching.

"He is unharmed," she hastened to add, relieved by Mr. Sullivan's reaction.

"Thank God," murmured her father.

"Where did it happen?" the earl questioned.

"In the meadow between the rectory and the woods. Deborah, the countess, and Lady Phillippa were with him."

"His lordship will have to be sent elsewhere to preserve his safety," Dunstan told them. "But first we shall ride to Pergrine's."

Chapter XIV

"Excuse me, my ladies." Dunstan bowed to the dowagers. "Mrs. Durham, Miss Durham." He included them all. "But I must deprive you of his lordship's presence. A matter of grave importance has arisen. My lord." He motioned for Lin to move to the door.

Hearing the urgency in his cousin's voice, Sullivan rose at once. "Till later this eve," he said, bowing and leaving the room, the earl hard on his heels.

"What is this about?" Lin asked when they reached the privacy of the bedchamber. "No," he spoke animatedly, "first let me tell you that this switching of identities must end."

"I know about the second attempt, Lin. I mean for you to depart from here in the morn. For your own protection," he added at his cousin's surprised look.

"That is not what I was speaking about." Lin reddened slightly. "I wish to propose to Miss Durham . . . to Deborah. I cannot as long as she believes me an earl."

"Why not tell her the truth after you wed?" Dunstan returned with his characteristic humour.

"You are impossible, Cris," Sullivan snapped. "Have you never cared what someone thought of you? Deborah may hate me when she learns she has been deceived."

Sudden seriousness crossed the earl's features. "If she loves you, it will not matter that you have no title. As for myself, there is something far more important than personal wishes at hand now. Do you feel you could ride a short distance?"

"What has that to do with . . . ?"

"I'll explain as we go." Dunstan tossed Lin his hat and grabbed his own. "We ride to see Lord Pergrine."

"How much longer must we sit here?" Lin questioned, dismounting. "We must see Pergrine on a matter more important than personal wishes," he mimicked the earl. "How is sitting in a clump of trees helping those two men you spoke of?"

"You shall see. All you have to do is agree to everything I say when we return to the rectory. We'll go in a few moments."

Another half hour passed; darkness fell. An owl hooted twice.

"We can go now," Dunstan said, untying their mounts and leading them from the cluster of trees. "Remember: agree to what I say. Plead fatigue as soon as my words end and request my assistance in retiring. No questions, Lin. Not yet."

"Bedlam or Newgate," Sullivan muttered as he swung into the saddle. "The man must be headed for one or the other."

"A delay has been arranged, Reverend Durham," Dunstan said as he and his cousin sat with the rector in the library. "Lord Pergrine has agreed to investigate the matter more fully."

"Can his lordship not speak of what passed between Lord Pergrine and himself?" Durham asked, puzzling over what he read as alarm in Dunstan's features at Sullivan's words.

"Cris speaks the truth," Lin said, prompted by a nod from the earl. "He was with me when I met with Pergrine. Do excuse me." He rose. "I am very fatigued from the day's activities. Cris, come and assist me." He turned to the door, unable to meet Durham's eyes.

"Good eve, Reverend," Dunstan said, rising. "My cousin must be abed. I trust you are satisfied with the results of our meeting with Pergrine?"

"You are certain the men are not to be hanged in the morn?"

"Very certain," Dunstan said, extending his hand, his eyes not wavering from Durham's.

"Then I am well pleased. Good eve to you."

"Till morn," the earl nodded and followed Lin.

Lady Brienne tossed uneasily in her bed. Sleep had not come quickly after the events of the day, nor was it deep. A board creaking alarmingly close brought her to instant wakefulness. She groped for the knitting needles she had kept beneath her pillow since Lin had first been wounded.

The full-mooned night sent a stream of light through the windows into the baroness's chamber, revealing two hulking shadows when she slowly opened one eye. Stealthily, they moved towards her bed. Forcing herself to remain motionless, she wondered if the ghost of Malvern had brought a friend.

A hand reached towards her.

"Hold fast," she said crisply, putting a knitting needle to the unknown's chest.

"What in God's name are you doing with a rapier?" Lady Imogene gasped, jumping back from the stab.

"Raspberries," swore the marchioness. "Brienne, have you gone mad?" She pushed the knitting needle aside. "Light the lamp, Imogene," she ordered.

"What do you mean by skulking about?" the baroness demanded. "How was I to know it was you? 'Pon my soul, I didn't have the ten years to spare that you've frightened from me this night." She laid a hand to her brow. "What time of night is it?" She jerked upright and fumbled for the timepiece on her bedside table.

"It is nearing three," the marchioness told her, taking the lamp from the countess. "Close the shutters," she instructed.

"Light the lamp, close the shutters," Lady Imogene muttered.

"Quiet, Imogene. Why are you two prowling about disturbing my sleep?" The baroness straightened her bedcovers as she stared comdemningly at them.

"Brienne," Lady Phillippa sat on the foot of the bed, "you will never guess whom I saw leaving the rectory shortly after we retired."

"Malvern's ghost?"

The marchioness frowned. "I suppose you consider that a jest? It was Mr. Sullivan. I have been awaiting his return. Immy has been helping me stay awake," she ended pertly.

"And now I am to keep you both alert, I suppose?"

149

"Oh, no. We just wished to discuss your idea about Enoch and Sarita."

The countess pulled a chair beside the bed and sat down. "There must be some way to reconcile the pair."

"Enoch is totally smitten with Deborah. That is a simple, unalterable fact. Do you refuse to recognize it?" the baroness asked.

"We do . . . we do concede there is a bit of truth to what you say," Lady Phillippa reluctantly agreed. "But truly, Brienne, could we not do better than a secretary for Sarita? She cannot have . . ."

"Phillippa," Lady Brienne scolded. "Of all people I would not expect to hear such nonsense from you. Did not your own daughter wed a nabob from India? I suggest you two step aside and leave these young people to decide for themselves whom they will marry."

"Such jibberish." Lady Imogene shook her grey curls. "Next you will have us believe all young people should choose their own spouses."

"Did you not?" Lady Brienne retorted, effectively ending the argument.

"But," the baroness continued, "I am intrigued by Mr. Sullivan's behaviour. If he is to marry Sarita, we must be certain he is of good character. Now, stealing out at this time of night is definitely unacceptable." She shook her finger at the two dowagers.

"Do you have an idea, Brienne?" the sisters asked expectantly, their eyes twinkling merrily at the prospect.

"Fetch me my slippers," the baroness commanded. "and my dressing gown." Once these were on and her sleeping bonnet adjusted, she took a firm hold on the knitting needles and blew out the lamp.

"What are we going to do?" Lady Phillippa asked excitedly.

"Follow me . . . quietly. Imogene, raise your skirts. We don't want you stumbling in the dark. Carefully now," she whispered. "We mustn't wake anyone."

Slowly the elderly trio edged their way through the corridor, down the stairs, and into the kitchen.

"You don't mean for us to go . . . go out?" the countess whispered nervously. "In the dark?"

"How else are we to catch Mr. Sullivan?"

"But he must enter here," Lady Phillippa added to Imogene's protest.

"Last week while in the garden I was contemplating the ivy growing so industriously beneath Enoch's and Mr. Sullivan's windows and noticed a few dying sprigs. I thought it was odd, but 'tis not so odd if someone has been climbing that wall."

"From the rectory's upper storey?" the countess asked as the baroness led the way out the kitchen door.

"He does look quite capable of such an action," the marchioness pondered aloud as they entered the garden. "But why are you using that strange tone when you speak of Mr. Sullivan, Brienne?"

"Later. For now let us position ourselves facing that window. Come." She waved the two towards the concealing shrubbery.

"My, the grass is damp. My slippers shall be ruined," the countess grumbled.

"Oh, Immy, forget about the slippers. This is so exciting." Lady Phillippa lightly clapped her hands.

"Both of you hush," hissed the baroness. "Get behind these shrubs. No, Imogene, that one's too small for you. Philly, your mobcap is hanging on that branch. Fetch it before someone sees it."

"Someone?" quaked the countess, moving to a different shrub. "You . . . you don't expect anyone but Mr. Sullivan, do you, Brienne? Could Malvern's ghost be about?"

"Oh, be quiet. Such nonsense. Wait, I thought I heard something." Lady Brienne waved for them to crouch down.

Coming from the woods, Dunstan glanced hurriedly over the landscape, then dashed for the rectory. Edging along the east wall in the garden, the sound of someone stirring in the stables caused him to dive beneath the closest shrub. A dampened cloth covered his face; he swallowed hard as he felt a pointed blade in his back and realized he was looking into the ruffling of the lower hem of a nightdress.

"Quiet!" Someone whispered.

All remained as they were until the stable door thudded shut once more.

Dunstan's eyes travelled upward. "What a delightful nightdress, Lady Phillippa," he said. "I truly regret not discovering it in a more . . . appropriate place," he bantered.

"Enough of your smooth words, Mr. Sullivan." Lady Brienne prodded him with the knitting needle.

"Baroness Mickle, if you would kindly remove your blade . . ."

"Not until your answers satisfy, Mr. Sullivan. Your

152

evening expedition is enough to raise curiosity, but could you perhaps explain Lady Devereau's description of yourself? You see, in a missive from that dear woman received just this day, she wrote: 'Mr. Sullivan is a tall, thin man of nervous habit, although he can be perfectly calm and wonderfully astute in business matters.' "

"Lady Devereau is a most charming woman . . ." he began.

"Might I mention," the baroness interrupted, jabbing him sharply, "that it was rumoured this same lady was, shall we say, briefly involved with Lord Dunstan. I believe she mentioned something about my nephew's 'terribly broad shoulders and ghastly thrilling locks.' A bit overdone, wouldn't you say, Mr. Sullivan?"

"You mean he is Enoch?" the countess asked indignantly. "But . . ."

"Brienne, you must be wrong," Lady Phillippa protested.

"Ladies. Your ladyships." Dunstan waved the white kerchief he had managed to free from his pocket. "Might we discuss this in a more . . . comfortable position?"

"Goodness, Brienne, if he is Enoch, let him rise." The marchioness took Dunstan's hand to assist him.

"Knitting needles?" He arched an eyebrow upon seeing what the baroness held.

"But quite as effective as a rapier."

"I definitely shall not argue . . . aunt. Not with them still in your hands." He bowed and then, much to her surprise, hugged her.

"Truly, Enoch," she scolded, straightening her

mobcap as he released her, but the moonlight revealed her delight.

" 'Tis with some hesitation, but I must protest," Dunstan said with grave reproach. " 'Tis Cris or Crispin I answer to among my closest friends."

"Crispin? Ah, yes, your head of curls." Lady Phillippa laughed quietly.

"But . . . but what of him?" the countess asked, pointing to the window above.

"He is Mr. Sullivan," Lady Brienne explained, shaking her head at the countess's slowness. "And we will hear the reason for this . . ."

"Aunts," the earl interrupted, "you have found me out, but no one else must know. Life and death for more than one depend upon that." He considered how much to reveal to them. " 'Tis not a game I play at. Friends and country are involved. Swear you shall tell no one." His voice hardened.

"We have not. We shall not," the baroness answered, her sisters nodding their assent.

"I can tell you no more. Let us turn to our beds. Would any of ye be wishin' ta join me?" he asked mischievously, motioning to the trellis.

"Now wouldn't you be surprised to have us?" Lady Brienne threw back her shoulders. "We have done it in the past, but I suppose we wouldn't want to frighten poor Lord Enoch to an early grave, would we, sisters?"

"Certainly not. Decidedly not," the countess answered hurriedly.

"Come, Brienne." The marchioness took her sister's arm and began marching her towards the rear of the rectory before anything further could be said.

With a smiling salute, Dunstan began his climb up the trellis, giving a huge sigh of relief as he dragged himself into the room above. "Methinks my aunts are a greater danger than Pergrine," he muttered as he tiredly pulled off his coat. "And all four will descend upon us in the morn."

Chapter XV

"Cris, we cannot just leave. Not without explanations," Lin continued to protest at dawn the next morning.

"I have a note telling Reverend Durham of a business matter which requires our immediate attention," Dunstan told him as he finished his packing and buckled the small portmanteau's straps.

"I must explain to Deborah—Miss Durham. I must tell her the truth."

"That cannot be done. For now let us remove you to safety."

Lin sat on the chair near the bed. "I refuse to go."

"Now, Lin, you know someone suspects that I . . ." He threw his hands in the air. "You know that I never would have changed identities with you if I had thought it would involve danger. I don't want anything to happen to you."

"But I cannot leave without telling Deborah. What if she learned the truth while we were gone? Why, she would never speak to me again." He rose and put a hand on the earl's shoulder. "What are you involved in, Cris? Since I have become a target, I have the right to know."

"The knowledge would only endanger you further."

Lin's lips pressed into a stubborn line as he folded his arms.

Dunstan studied his cousin for a moment. "You have heard that Napoleon is assembling an invasion force directly across the Channel from Hastings at Boulogne. Some of his landing craft are already completed. The War Ministry has learned that someone in this area is sending reports on troop numbers and movements, shore fortifications and similar information directly to Napoleon. I am hear to learn who that man is," Dunstan ended softly.

"You . . . ?" Lin began. "But all those rumours of amourous escapades . . ."

"At times a ruse. At times . . ." Dunstan shrugged, trying to lighten his cousin's grim looks.

"But we both could be killed if the informer believes we know . . ."

"Exactly. Now will you come?" Relief filled the earl's voice.

"No."

"Lin, I shall brook no . . ."

"You must understand. I see the danger, but I cannot abandon Deborah. No, I must remain."

Dunstan's look challenged him.

"I mean to wed the chit, Cris, if she will have me after the explanations are done. Her heart is devilish well set on being a countess." He fingered his cravat nervously.

A wry grin came to the earl's lips. "I am sorry, Lin. Had I known . . ."

"There are no regrets on my part. It is"—he grimaced apologetically—"reassuring to learn you are not . . ."

157

"Entirely frivolous," Dunstan finished for him. "We both have learned a great deal about one another." He held out his hand. They shook solemnly. "Now I must go to Hastings. Don't ask why. It's to your protection not to know. I may be gone two, three days. I will leave the explanation of my absence to you. Do not provide too broad a target," he joked lightly as he picked up the portmanteau. Halting at the door, he admonished once again. "No one is to be told."

"I understand, Cris. God speed your return."

"How did he manage it?" Lady Imogene fretted as the dowagers strolled in the garden in early morn. "Why, he never explained anything."

"If you two had not been so fearful of having to climb a simple trellis, I could have questioned him," the baroness returned. "He is wily, but then he is our nephew," she nodded, smiling.

"But how are we to learn anything? Imagine, stealing away so early in the morn." Lady Phillippa pursed her lips.

"He probably realized you two would now direct all your matchmaking efforts at him," Lady Brienne countered with a laugh, then grew serious. "No, the surprise is that he left Enoch here to face the danger alone."

"You mean Mr. Sullivan," the countess retorted, still angry at the trick. "How ungentlemanly of them to do such a thing."

"It would be best to continue as we have or we shall let the secret out," the baroness corrected her. "Until we know the reason for this subterfuge, let's not damage it. Where is everyone this morn?" Her eyes swept the open meadow before them.

"Reverend Durham left just as we were rising. I imagine he went to see those two unfortunate men. Sarita has gone with a basket of food to the Widow Trumbull, and Deborah and Enoch are in the solarium . . . with Mrs. Durham as chaperone." Lady Imogene rattled the list off with ease.

The other two eyed her appraisingly.

"Have I forgotten someone? Oh, Tessy. She is preparing . . ."

"No, no," the other two laughed. "Enough."

The sound of approaching horsemen drew their eyes to the meadow.

"Why, they are coming here," Lady Phillippa exclaimed and put her hand fearfully to her heart. "What could they want?"

Hurrying, the dowagers reached the front of the rectory as the horsemen reined to a halt. "Open the doors," the surly leader demanded, jumping down. "We mean to find the Trumbulls if we have to ransack the place."

"Mademoiselle Durham . . . Sarita. May I not walk with you?" Pierre Mandel called to her as she hurried along the path towards the rectory. "I shall carry that basket for you," he said, reaching her side.

"It is empty and very light," she said, refusing to give it up. "I must return home quickly," she added, her steps not slowing.

"You have heard then?" Mandel questioned. "Are you not pleased?"

"Of what do you speak, *monsieur?*" Sarita ignored the intimacy of his tone.

"The freeing of the Trumbull brothers. I thought such an act would please you greatly." He eyed her appraisingly, his tone filled with disappointment.

"It pleases me very much, but what interest do you have . . . ? You didn't help them, did you?" she asked doubtfully.

"Why do you question it, *mademoiselle?* Do you think me so spineless that I would not aid them?" he asked, pretending to be hurt.

"Of course not. It is just that you and Lord Pergrine . . ."

"It is for my father that I maintain a pretense of being friendly with the man."

"But your father dislikes the . . ."

"He does not understand the ways of the world. *Non,* his head is in his flowers." Mandel took one of Sarita's hands; his eyes swept over her petite form appreciatively. "You are pleased, are you not?" He reached to touch her dark curls.

A chill ran through her as his tone caressed her. "I believe it was the right thing to do, *monsieur.*"

"Pierre, please."

"Pierre," she returned frigidly. "But are you not in danger?" she asked, managing to free her hand from his clammy hold.

"*Non.* No one but you knows that I freed them, and *certainement* I need not fear you shall tell anyone, *n'est-ce pas?*"

"You know I wouldn't, but freeing the Trumbull brothers really wasn't necessary. Lord Dunstan and Mr. Sullivan spoke with Lord Pergrine last eve, and he was going to delay taking any action," Sarita told him proudly.

"Who told you this?" Mandel's eyes narrowed.

"Why . . ."

"Sullivan again," the Frenchman spat. "No one called on Lord Pergrine last eve. I was watching the manor myself . . . biding my time for the most opportune moment."

Sarita shook her head in disbelief.

"Ask Monsieur Sullivan himself."

"I cannot. He has gone away on business," she returned numbly.

"Ah, the *couard*. He realized the truth would be made known," Pierre said, a triumphant gleam in his eye.

"There must be some explanation," Sarita countered.

"Only the truth. Listen to me, *m'amie*. I have told you what the man is. This proves my words." Confidence oiled his voice. "You know, my sweet, Father is very fond of you. It would please him very much if we were to . . ."

"I must go, Pierre." Sarita began to step away, but he caught her arm.

"They have done no damage. There is no need to rush," he leered.

"What do you mean?"

"The men who searched for the Trumbulls, of course."

"The rectory? Mother . . ." She jerked free and bolted down the path.

Mandel's eyes followed her hungrily. "*Oui*, the poor mother. She needn't worry about her daughter much longer. How fortune smiles on me with Monsieur Sullivan's absence."

"You are certain of this information." Dunstan, unrecognizable in tattered sailor's garb with a heavy stubble on his face, leaned across the table in the dimly lit ale house.

Billy nodded grimly.

The earl whistled.

"The word is he'll come with his master, Lord Gerard, who has been invited to Pergrine Manor."

"What reason has been given for the invitation?"

"His lordship invited Lord Gerard so he could relax away from the strain of the War Office," Billy clipped softly.

"Then Pergrine is involved."

"The Admiralty believes someone else is also, someone who knows the French coast well and speaks the language."

"Mandell!" Dunstan's fist clenched.

"We have no names. It is for you to learn them."

"Is Gerard suspected in this?"

"No, only his man Finley. Nor is it believed he would accept an accusation against his man. That is why you must handle it. They are uncertain which papers Finley has managed to copy, but Lord Gerard has access to the most confidential listings."

"The papers will be brought with him. If only we knew their intent. Pergrine is no fool. He must realize he cannot remain undetected." Dunstan rubbed a hand calculatingly across his rough beard. "See if you can find any rumours of expected crossings on the

Channel within the next week to ten days. They will have to make their move soon."

"Aye, but 'tis dangerous. How fares his lordship?"

"Better than one might suppose, for a partridge in the midst of hunting season," the earl quipped. "Direct the men you spoke of to come to the Anchor and Sail at midnight." He rose.

Billy nodded in farewell and watched him till he was gone. Rising, he proceeded to his own rendezvous.

A soft knock stiffened Lady Brienne as she was about to get into bed. "Enter," she snapped, her temper still riled by the actions of Pergrine's searchers.

Sarita paused in the doorway, her smallness emphasized by her full, white nightdress, her black hair framing her pert face. The large dark eyes bespoke a vulnerability the baroness had not noted before. "I beg your pardon for disturbing you so late," she said.

"Well, child, it is done. Close the door and tell me what it is you wish." Lady Brienne tried to temper her words, sensing the young woman's hesitancy.

"You see, you are the oldest . . . I mean the most sensible . . ." Sarita shook her head, her hands clenched.

"I believe I understand what you are trying to say," the baroness told her softly. "Come. Sit. Tell me what troubles you."

A heavy sigh came as Sarita sat down. "You must realize by now that Mother refuses to deal with anything distressing. She retreats into her own world at times . . . so I have only Father to turn to. But in this matter I cannot help but feel he would . . ."

She shrugged awkwardly. "Excuse me." Sarita rose abruptly and made for the door.

"Come back, child. I do not intend to lose an entire night's sleep pondering on what you intended to speak of. Does it concern Mr. Sullivan?"

The young woman whirled to face the baroness. "Is it so plain?"

"I suppose he has been paying court to you?"

"Oh, no. I don't think so. Not that I wouldn't wish him to, or so I thought," Sarita admitted with her customary frankness, returning to the chair and slowly sitting.

"So you thought? What has happened to alter this?" Lady Brienne studied her sharply. "Speak, child."

"It was Pierre," Sarita burst out, her inner turmoil surfacing. "He claims that he set the Trumbull brothers free and that Mr. Sullivan and Lord Dunstan never went to see Lord Pergrine last eve. He says Cris is a coward and has run away because he knows he will be found out." Doubt and anger mingled in her words.

"You believe this?" Lady Brienne challenged, bristling.

"I do not want to, my heart tells me not to, but there is so much that is . . . baffling about Mr. Sullivan." Sarita jumped up. "Oh, I am a fool. I don't even know if he cares for me." She blushed a bright red.

"But you care for him?" The baroness cocked her head, holding back her smile.

"I am concerned for his safety. Pierre," she shivered, "well, he seems to hate Mr. Sullivan. Why would Cris leave without saying anything to anyone . . . or at least to me if he cared? Even Lord Dunstan has avoided me all day. It is much a muddle."

"I agree, and a muddle not easily understood. I believe it is highly unlikely that Monsieur Mandel had anything to do with freeing the Trumbulls. He is far too involved with himself to care for others . . . unless there was something to his benefit in it." She noticed Sarita's sudden repulsion. "Is there something you have not told me?"

"Pierre said . . . said he did it to please me, that his father wished us to wed."

"Has he made improper advances?" Lady Brienne's eyes hardened.

"No. No, I have always stayed as far from him as I could. There is something about the way he looks at me." She shivered again.

"I understand," the baroness told her. "You do well to avoid him. In the future we shall have a keener watch on Monsieur Mandel. But, calm your doubts about Mr. Sullivan. He is certain to return and explain everything."

"It is so useless. With Mother . . ."

"Sarita! Sarita!" Deborah's excited voice interrupted her, taking both women to the door. "What are we to do?" she asked. "Lady Dunstan has arrived and is in hysterics. She is shouting at Father, and Lord Enoch is nowhere to be found!"

Chapter XVI

"Henrietta, calm yourself," Lady Brienne commanded, striding into the library where her sister was berating Reverend Durham. Sarita followed close behind.

"What have you done with my son?" Lady Dunstan demanded, swinging to face the baroness. "How could you harm him? I shall see that all of you are brought to justice," she ranted. "Where are you going? Put that vase down," she said, treading upon the baroness's heels as the other calmly walked from her sister to a sidetable. "Put that vase down and listen to me."

Lady Brienne ignored her and casually removed the daisies from the vase. "Will you listen, Henrietta?" she asked carefully, her look telegraphing her intent.

"I would gladly listen if only you will tell me what has happened to my son. Put that vase down, I say." Annoyance edged the anger in her tone. "Have you gone daft? Really, Reverend Durham," she stamped her foot as she turned to him, "you must make her explain what has become of . . ." Lady Dunstan's words ended as the baroness dumped the vase of water over her.

"Take this." Lady Brienne offered her kerchief while the rector looked on the scene in utter amazement. "You always did carry on far too much, Henrietta. What is the reason for this impetuous visit?" She raised the vase in her hand, halting a threatened renewal of the outburst.

Lady Phillippa burst into the library. "Why, Henrietta, what has happened? You poor dear," the marchioness clucked, putting her arm about her sister.

"Refill this." Lady Brienne handed the vase to the countess as she padded onto the scene.

"Brienne, you are the most obnoxious . . ." Lady Dunstan began.

"Ladies, ladies." Reverend Durham stepped forward. "Let us put aside personal differences for Lord Dunstan's sake."

"Is he truly to be found?" the baroness asked.

"It is all your fault, you overstarched twig," the earl's mother began, but was again silenced, this time by the squeeze Lady Phillippa gave her. "Well, you did invite him here." Tears welled up in her eyes. "Oh, Reverend Durham, what has happened? You say my son can't be found."

"We must remain calm, Lady Dunstan. Please, won't all of you take a seat while I tell the little I know?" He motioned for them to sit and then noticed Deborah's white face peering into the room. "Has your mother heard of his lordship's absence?" he asked concernedly.

"No, she sleeps," came the faint reply.

"Then come in, child," he said gently. Waiting until Deborah had sat down, the rector paced to the massive bookcase lining the west wall and turned. "Quite simply, Lord Dunstan excused himself less than an hour ago, saying he wished to walk in the garden a bit before retiring. I had no idea anything was amiss until your arrival." He nodded at Lady Dunstan.

"You have searched his bedchamber? The solarium? What of the garden?" the baroness asked, her calmness belying her inner fears.

Reverend Durham nodded. "To no avail."

"But could he not have decided to walk farther . . . perhaps into the woods?" Deborah asked hopefully, her hands clenched and white-knuckled in her lap.

"We may hope that, but I fear the worse," her father returned, shaking his head.

"Kidnapped," Lady Brienne put in matter-of-factly.

"Or worse still," agreed the rector as Lady Dunstan began to sob.

"Now yer lordship, 'ope this convinces ye to tell us how much ye heard and where ye sent yer man." The burly figure struck Lin several blows to the ribs as two other men held him firmly between them. He sagged in their hold. "Now where be Sullivan?" his tormentor demanded.

"Told you," Lin gasped. "In . . . Hastings . . . on business."

Angrily the man yanked Lin's drooping head up. He sent his fist against the already bruised jaw with sickening force.

"Ye ain't be gettin' nothin' from 'im," said a voice from the shadows. One of the two that held Lin laughed sourly, letting go his hold.

A tall, thin figure emerged into the cave's dim light

as Lin fell to the floor. "Tie him. Where did you say you found him?"

"Followed us 'e did. Must 'ave seen 'Al's light. Told 'im not ta use it. Came from the rectory like 'e owned the woods. Think 'e 'eard us talkin' 'about the shipment."

"Fools. I told you to be careful! Take the men to the usual meeting place. The boat should be in soon, and someone has to be there."

"Why don't we take 'im with us? Fine fishbait 'e'd make." The burly man prodded Lin's prone form roughly with his scuffed boot.

"He may yet prove useful. If not, you may use him for what you like. Now go, and no more mistakes or you'll become fishbait." The other smiled evilly, then turned and stalked out.

"Ye'd better be careful yerself," the rough man sneered at the other's back. "There's them that don't like yer highhanded ways. Ye 'eard," he snapped at his cohorts. "Get this un' tied. Drag 'im to the back of the cave." He gave Lin a kick as he passed him.

"What are we to do, Brienne?" Lady Imogene asked nervously as she joined her two sisters in the garden. "Whatever are we to do?"

"Calm yourself, Immy," Lady Phillippa urged. "You'll have palpitations if you don't."

"A pother on that," she waved agitatedly at the marchioness. "Crispin shall be returning and what will we do . . . or if Reverend Durham and Mr. Traunt find Lord Enoch . . . what then? Either way Henrietta shall know. My, what a scene we shall have then. Oh, and after he said it was so important that no one know." She halted for sheer lack of breath.

"Sit down, Imogene," Lady Brienne commanded. "There is a problem, I agree, but I am equally certain we shall manage it. If Crispin is as knowledgeable as I believe, he will not walk into the midst of us without some warning. For now, we must play the worried aunts. In truth, I do fear for Lord Enoch."

"You? Care? For someone other than yourself?" Lady Dunstan's icy tone froze the three.

"Henrietta." The marchioness stepped towards her, but Lady Brienne's arm stopped her.

"There is no reason we cannot behave in a reasonably civilized manner," the baroness pointedly noted.

"No reason," Lady Henrietta returned coldly.

"We *are* distressed at Lord Enoch's disappearance. Very distressed." Lady Brienne allowed a hint of her concern to show.

"Enoch. Why does everyone call him Enoch?" Lady Dunstan's features contorted as she tried to stave off a bout of tears. "My dear Crispin. What has become of him?" Her eyes begged an answer of Lady Brienne. "Shall I ever see my mischievous lad again?"

"I am certain you shall." Lady Brienne reached out consolingly. "Reverend Durham and Mr. Traunt have many men searching." She sought to reassure her.

"But why would anyone want to harm him?" Lady Henrietta took the baroness's arm, her concern for her son dwarfing the memory of their past quarrels.

"There is oft much one does not know about sons . . . or nephews," Lady Brienne answered carefully.

"This would not have happened if he had wed as I wished," the earl's mother continued, unhearing. "I have reached my wits' end with him. Do you know, I came here actually hoping you had been successful?" She looked to Lady Phillippa. "I was even willing to accept anyone, provided, of course, that she was of the gentry."

"Of course," the baroness controlled her remark.

"Do you mean that?" the marchioness asked cautiously. "I mean, you would not object if he wished to wed. . . . Well, what if he wished to wed one of Reverend Durham's daughters?"

"One of the rector's . . . ? Why, you don't mean . . . ?"

"He could always choose one of those garish merchants' daughters. Like the Viscount of Harrow did just last month," the countess interjected.

"And rumours of his reputation with ladies of doubtful repute are widespread," Lady Brienne noted.

Lady Dunstan shrugged in surrender. "He is hopeless. I will be fortunate if he, indeed, ever marries."

"But you would not discourage a match with Miss Durham?" Lady Phillippa persisted.

"Have you managed to interest him in one of them?" Lady Dunstan asked suspiciously and burst into tears. "What use is this foolish chatter? What if he is . . . dead?" she sobbed.

In the rectory's kitchen a like scene was being played. Deborah and Sarita had been finishing the morning's dishes when the younger fumbled and dropped a plate, smashing it to pieces.

"A broken plate is nothing to shed such tears over, Debs," Sarita told her sister as she bent to help her pick up the pieces.

"I'm not . . . crying . . . over the . . . plate." Deborah rasied tear-flooded eyes to her sister's. "Do you think . . . think he still lives?" Her lower lip trembled.

"Lord Enoch? Of course." Sarita drew her sister to her as she broke into fresh sobs. "Do you wish to be a countess that badly?" she asked.

Drawing back abruptly, Deborah daubed at her eyes. "Do you think so poorly of me that you can ask that?" She blew her nose soundly. "I don't care if I never become a countess if only Lord Enoch is returned unharmed," she sniffed. "I know you think I dwell only on frippery and geegaws, Sarry, but this is different. Enoch is so . . . special. I do believe I love him."

"Oh, Debs." Sarita opened her arms and the two embraced. "If Clem and Father do not find him, I know Mr. Sullivan will."

"You care for Mr. Sullivan, don't you, Sarry?" Deborah questioned, recovered enough to study her sister closely.

"We had better get this plate taken care of before Tessy returns," the other dodged the question.

"What have you done? Another plate?" Tessy towered over them, hands on hips. Suddenly she softened. "Well, 'tis to be understood with his lordship missing and his mother coming on us like she did. I'll see to

172

this. That young Frenchman's out in the garden wishing to see you, Miss Sarita. Go on now."

"You go, Deborah. I'll help finish this," she answered quickly.

"Won't do, miss. Your mother said to send you both. So off with you." Tessy shooed them from the kitchen.

"Why don't you like Mr. Mandel?" Deborah asked as they walked through the Hall.

"I think very highly of Monsieur Mandel," Sarita tossed back lightly.

"I mean Pierre. Why, the Bradly girls and even Laura Simpson would love to have him pay court to them as much as he does to you."

"I have never encouraged him," she snapped.

"I didn't mean . . ."

"I'm sorry, Debs. It's just that I . . . I don't care for Pierre. Let's hurry. Perhaps he has word of Lord Enoch," she said, thinking to change the course of the conversation.

"My goodness, Deborah, such hoydenish behaviour," Mrs. Durham reprimanded her youngest as she ran up to the small group in the garden.

"Tessy said Mr. Mandel was here and I thought perhaps"—she turned eagerly to him—"that you might have news of Lord . . . Dunstan."

"*Je regrette,* I am sorry, *mademoiselle,* but I carry no such tidings." He bowed, his expression contrite, "I fear my news is much at odds with your present circumstances"—his motion took in all—"for I bring invitations to Lord Pergrine's grand ball."

Chapter XVII

"Lord Pergrine has invited all of us?" Sarita questioned dubiously.

"*Oui*. Her ladyship especially wishes you to come." Mandel bowed to the dowagers. "It is to be a *grande célébration*.

"I don't know. I don't know what to say," Mrs. Durham said nervously. "Reverend Durham and Lord Pergrine have been at such . . . Well, you know they have not agreed on . . . Oh dear, what shall we do?" She looked at Sarita.

"Lord Pergrine desired me to tell you he feels that in this time of trouble perhaps a new beginning can be made, that the seeds of understanding can be sown between him and your husband," the Frenchman purred smoothly, convincingly. "One should not let such an opportunity pass. Think of the good it could do for the people if Lord Pergrine chose to be your husband's sponsor once more."

"Mother, how can you even consider going to a ball at that man's home? Especially when Lord Enoch may be . . ." Deborah threw her hands to her face and ran sobbing to the rectory.

"I agree most heartily with Miss Durham," Lady Dunstan said acidly. "That you are even thinking of going is quite telling." Throwing her head back haughtily, she angrily followed Deborah.

"My sister is quite naturally upset at this time," Lady Brienne told Mandel with a pleading smile. "We shall gladly accept Lord Pergrine's kind invitation."

"Lady Brienne," Sarita burst forth, "surely . . ."

The baroness's icy stare stilled the argument on the young woman's lips. "You may assure Lady Pergrine that my sisters and I shall be there," said the baroness. She nodded towards a frowning Lady Imogene and a distressed Lady Phillippa.

"And you?" Mandel's eyes flashed back to Sarita.

"That shall be decided later," the baroness told him, taking his arm. "Walk with me. I must know what the usual dress is at these country affairs." She spoke easily as she led him a short distance from the group.

The countess and Lady Phillippa exchanged questioning looks as they took in this unusual conversation from Lady Brienne, who in selecting her own toilette had never before shown the least consideration for what others wore.

"My, my," Mrs. Durham mumbled, her composure deeply shaken.

"Mother, calm yourself," said Sarita. "Let us see to luncheon for our guests."

"Yes, of course," her head bobbed. "Yes," she spoke aloud, looking at no one as she turned and walked slowly away.

Concern filled Sarita as she followed her, glancing back towards the baroness and Mandel.

Pierre caught her look, quickly excused himself with a bow, and hastened to her side. "A message from my father, *ma chérie*," he said quietly. "He says you will understand this." Mandel posed affectedly for a moment and then recited, " 'The moon will be high; the time is nigh. The star is about to burst in the sky.' You *comprenez* this?"

Sarita shook her head slowly, then understanding flashed. "Of course," she smiled, a hint of excitement in her voice.

"If only you would look this way for me." He reached out to touch her cheek.

The baroness joined them at this moment and deftly took hold of Pierre's arm. "How naughty of you," she twittered. "You see Miss Durham often, but we visit for only a brief time. 'Tis said that if we please some, others will also be pleased." She nodded meaningfully at Sarita.

"*Oui,* as you say," he agreed with a sly smile.

"You may go and help your mother," Lady Brienne instructed Sarita, who walked away with deliberate steps, undecided whether to be thankful for being rescued or angry at the baroness's manner.

"You will see that the *mademoiselle* attends the ball?" Mandel's lips brushed Lady Brienne's hand.

"Of course, *monsieur*. But could you not describe some of the guests we shall meet?" she asked affectedly. "It is so much more interesting to be able to recognize a few of the more important people. It impresses them bloody well, too," she added with a wink.

"*Oui,* my lady," he smiled. "The principal guest shall be Lord Gerard, a man easily known, being tall, jowl-faced . . . one certain of his own importance." Mandel began his descriptions, revealing much about others . . . and himself.

*　*　*

"Do you think the dowagers mean to go to the ball?" Deborah asked as the two sisters retired to their room after a long, fruitless day. "Surely their sensibilities forbid it? You heard Father tell them how widely they have searched and to no avail," she ended sadly, a tear trailing down her pale cheek.

Sarita sat on the bedside with her sister. "Don't cry again, Debs." She took her hand. "We will find Lord Enoch."

"But Father said . . ."

"He only meant that it would take more time to find Lord Dunstan than he had thought. No one knows the countryside like Clem, and when Mr. Sullivan returns, even on the morrow, they will find his lordship."

"Oh, Sarry, I've been such a fool. I'll never again look at . . . at Irish lace . . . or even think of Italian combs for my hair." She daubed at her eyes. "If only Enoch is found . . . unharmed." Deborah sniffed and blew her reddened nose. "You must learn a lesson from this, Sarry. If Mr. Sullivan pays court, seize the opportunity," she advised with wide-eyed seriousness.

"You know that with Mother's weakness of mind— her dependence—I could never leave," Sarita answered softly, studying her hands. She raised her chin determinedly. "Let us keep our worries with Lord Enoch for now," she laughed nervously and rose. "Don't be concerned if you hear someone come in during the night. I will be going out."

"What could you be doing at this time of night?" A

weak smile came to Deborah's lips. "It wouldn't be Pierre, would it?" she teased.

Sarita threw a pillow at her sister. "Do you advise me to encourage Monsieur Mandel as well?"

"The son or the father? You never . . ." Deborah burst into laughter at Sarita's look. "Oh, go to your plants and flowers . . ." She fell back on her bed as she caught a second pillow. Hugging the pillow close, Deborah renewed her prayers for Lord Enoch's safe return as the door closed behind Sarita.

"It is a matter of timing, Mademoiselle Sarita. An hour, longer perhaps. See . . . the petals begin to separate." Monsieur Mandel pointed to the pinkish-veined, swordlike petals just slightly apart on the bud. "Would it not be best if you waited here? I dislike you walking home alone in the dark, and I dare not leave. The drawings must be precise at each stage."

"Don't worry, *monsieur*. It is safe enough and best that I be in the rectory should Mother awake."

Deep concern came to his features. "These are uncertain times, *mademoiselle*. Think of what happened to Lord Enoch." He read the determination in her stance and shrugged. "God watch over your path," he said in farewell.

Deciding it would be faster to go home by means of a seldom-travelled path, instead of the usual one between the greenhouse and the rectory, Sarita hurried forward. The night light, however, was very poor and the path had become more overgrown than she recalled. The walking proved difficult.

I'd best return to the other path, she thought, and struck out at a right angle for it. A few paces off the track the murmur of voices coming towards her lurched her to a halt. Crouching, Sarita huddled next to a tree, hoping she would not be discovered.

The voices came closer, the words understandable.

"*Le Blatte* says they must have the troop number and movement information before more gold will be sent," a raspy whisper sounded.

"Do they know the costs I bear?" a second objected. "The plans are almost in our grasp. Do they wish to risk losing them? Tell *Le Blatte* I must have 4000 pounds for the final bribe. Without it we shall have gained nothing. And there must be assurances that a boat will be waiting if it proves necessary to depart suddenly."

"I can promise nothing, for it is getting too risky to keep a boat hovering in the coves. Last night a dozen men caught one of our craft, hidden as it was among the rocks. Luckily, it was only carrying brandy, but fortune will not always cause a last-minute change in cargo. It could well have been the gold or the muskets, which arrived tonight."

"Fortune is with me. Only a few days more and all I wish will be mine," the second bantered cockily as the two passed not ten yards from Sarita. "Napoleon will be *très généreux* for what I have accomplished."

Stifling a gasp as she caught a glimpse of this man's face, Sarita realized it was Pierre Mandel. Waiting until she could no longer hear the two, she rose and ran quickly to the well-trod path. Her headlong steps took her rapidly towards the rectory, and she did not pause until safely inside.

From his place beneath the shrubs in the garden where he had scrambled at the sound of running footsteps, Dunstan saw Sarita's pell-mell return and puzzled over it as he climbed the trellis to the upper storey. Edging along the stone ledge, he eased open a window and quickly slipped into the chamber. Despite what he had been told by Jervy, he made a quick check of the bedchamber, as if hoping to find Lin there.

A deep frown covered his features. First the raiding party had failed to net anything other than brandy, and now Lin had been kidnapped. Where was he and why was Sarita running as if the ghost of Malvern were after her? *Jervy,* he thought, *he may know what she is about. I wonder why he didn't mention it. I will have to contact him again.* Dunstan sat upon the large, canopied bed. But first some sleep, he told his tired body as he laid back on the inviting softness. His thoughts flew over all the possibilities concerning Lin and Sarita and settled on her image as he drifted to sleep.

A dog howling in the distance brought Dunstan abruptly to consciousness. He rose instantly and walked to the windows, scanning the garden and open meadow in the murky darkness. Nothing met his eyes. He slipped out the open window and down the trellis, drawn by an unfathomable need. Just as he touched the ground, the click of iron against iron sounded and he realized someone was using the kitchen door. The petite, gowned figure scurrying away from the rectory pawed at his heart. "Sarita," he whispered quietly and hurried to follow.

With an uneasy spirit Sarita began the return trip to Mandel's. The brief conversation she had over-heard had made sleep impossible. Pierre Mandel, a traitor . . . for that alone was what their talk of being rewarded by Napoleon could mean. But what could he know that would help the First Consul? Poor Monsieur Mandel. Her thoughts took another direction as she hurried along. This will break his heart. Should I tell him? No. Then Father? Doubts remained unresolved as the greenhouse loomed before her.

Entering, she made her way to Mandel's solitary light. Over his shoulder she took in the beauty he had waited so long to see. "Oh, it is simply marvelous, *monsieur*. All you said it would be," Sarita breathed as she continued gazing at the fully opened blossom, the glistening white of its interior enhanced by the delicate golden stamen within.

"*Oui, c'est magnifique.*" He paused in his sketching. "The perfect bloom that I have worked for. My drawings and report shall win the *grand* prize from the Academy in London. Then perhaps Pierre . . . Perhaps when we have the money it shall bring . . ." He halted, his eyes going back to the delicate, long-petaled flower that was as large as a saucer. "*C'est belle,*" he mused. "*Le cereus grandiflorus.* What a long journey from *Amérique* it has had. Señor Corata gave the tiny plant to Monsieur Trienne to give me when he sailed from the Spanish colonies two years ago. It may be the only one of its kind in England."

"I am so glad I was able to see it." Sarita smiled at his oft-told words. "Are you certain it will close by morn? I would so like the dowagers to see it."

"Those who have seen it say there will be nothing

but a limp glob of opaque pulp by morn," Mandel told her regretfully.

"So beautiful. How sad it has to be so brief."

"Blossoms are not the only things in life that are momentary. Many times happiness, too, must be snatched before it is gone," the old Frenchman said, putting his hand on Sarita's shoulder.

She mentally winced at the knowledge that she held about Pierre. "I suppose," she answered, aching for him. "I must go," she blurted, feeling tears coming to her eyes.

"*Oui.* I shall walk with you this time."

"There is no need. No, I am certain," she hurriedly assured him. *Adieu.*" With a wave of her hand, she left the old man glorying in the perfect blossom of the night-blooming cereus.

Sarita's heart pounded abnormally loudly in her ears as she walked along the the path, for it seemed every shadow held an unknown danger. Tears for Monsieur Mandel, for Deborah and Lord Enoch, and for herself, came to her eyes.

At the edge of the woods her fears became reality as a tallish, square form of a man blocked her path. In the pale moonlight her face blanched bone white. A scream lodged in her throat. She swayed.

"It is I . . . Cris," Dunstan's deep voice rang in welcome relief.

With a sob, she stepped into his open arms.

The earl held her tightly for a long, savoured moment, then gently eased her back and searched her small face. A large finger slowly traced a tear. "Why do you cry, my little one? I did not mean to startle you so. Forgive me?"

The relief, the warmth, drained from Sarita as she returned his gaze. Her eyes took in the rough growth of beard, the tattered, soiled garments he wore. "Why . . . ? What . . . ?" she stammered.

"My appearance is rather untoward." He grimaced uneasily. "But," the grimace turned to a teasing smile, "methinks it odd to find my love roaming the woods at such an hour."

Sarita's heart lurched at his words. "My love" echoed through her mind.

"Is it fear I read?" The earl drew her closer once more. "Do you not know I . . ." Words failed; his lips claimed hers.

An impulse to resist surged through Sarita. Her hands went to his chest to fend him off. She felt the strength of the man, a somehow comforting strength, and thought of Monsieur Mandel's words. Was this her chance to snatch at happiness? Slowly her hands relaxed, then stole softly about his neck.

A long moment later Dunstan drew back unwillingly, a wry smile on his lips. "If I would ask . . ." He paused and Sarita read a flash of uncertainty, "would you wed me freely, with no explanations?"

Loving mischief sparkled through the dampness in her eyes. "I would have no fewer questions than you."

"Would you marry me?" The earnestness of his tone gripped her.

Melancholy came to Sarita with reality's return. The impulse to answer as she wished was stifled. "If I were free, I would. With no questions asked."

Dunstan traced the line of her cheek lovingly, and softly kissed her lips. After a long gaze he shook himself, his hold eased. "Li . . . Lord Enoch . . . Where has he gone?" he asked, studying her closely.

"How could you know he is gone?" Sarita's eyes flew towards the rectory, a mound of darkness in the meadow before them.

"No questions," he returned, quashing his desire to explain.

Sarita studied the man before her appraisingly. That she loved him, she did not question. But he stood before her in the semblance of a rogue, a footpad. Who was he? Did she dare trust him with all she knew?

"What has happened to . . . his lordship?" Dunstan pressed her for an answer, firmly, gently.

"He has disappeared. Since late last eve. Father believes he has been kidnapped, perhaps murdered."

An invisible pain flickered over Dunstan's features.

"No one is certain," she hurried to explain. "You see, we had all retired to our rooms except for Father when Lady Dunstan arrived." Sarita paused as she felt a quiver go through him. "Her ladyship demanded to see the earl, but Father could not find him. We found only his hat in the garden."

"Damnation," the earl swore accusingly at himself.

"Father, Clem, and several other men searched all this day." She tried to comfort him, not knowing he was already privy to this information. Strangely, she felt relieved at the distress she saw and yet puzzled. "Do you know what has become of him?" she forced herself to ask.

"I have my suspicions," he returned curtly.

"Do you think he still lives?" she added softly.

"I pray it is so." His hand gripped hers painfully.

"For it is my doing if he has been harmed." He shook his head at her questioning plea. "I will walk you to the rectory," he said, taking her arm, moving forward slowly. "It wouldn't do for you to encounter anyone," he told her with a hollow laugh. They walked half the distance in silence, then Dunstan spoke again. "Will you ask the baroness to come to the brook just beyond the garden in the morn as soon as she rises?"

"If you wish . . ." Sarita answered slowly. "Will you not return to the rectory now?"

"What would your father have to say of the two of us, walking about unchaperoned at this hour?" A hint of humour edged his voice. "No," the seriousness was back, "I must ask you to have faith in me, no matter what circumstances bid you to believe. Have faith for just a short time longer." His eyes pleaded as he spoke softly. He paused; his mind flickered. "How has Lady Dunstan taken the news?"

"Rather badly. She accused Father of having been responsible for Lord Enoch's being shot and now of having done away with him. Lady Brienne tried to reason with her ladyship but ended by pouring a vase of water over her. It has all been so . . . odd," she sighed. "They do seem to have reconciled, and at least Lady Dunstan goes on well with Deborah. I do not envy my sister when Lord Enoch is found and they marry," she said without thinking.

"Truly?" Open humour filled Dunstan's voice and features.

"I did not mean that . . ." Sarita looked to his grin and was unaccountably angered. "You should know Lady Dunstan well enough to know what I mean."

"I know her ladyship well, indeed." He squeezed Sarita's hand. "And your words are not unfounded."

"Never mind," she returned sharply. "If you know her so well, you realize she would never approve of your dressing in such a hideous manner or of your prowling about as you evidently have been doing."

"No more than she would her son doing it," he countered lightly.

A strange quality in his voice tugged at Sarita's mind. She reached to touch his cheek.

Catching her hand, the earl brushed it with a kiss. "Tell no one but the baroness," he instructed. "It would be interesting to hear your explanation of how you encountered me," he teased, cocking his head.

"Your explanation would be equally fascinating."

"Is it a nagging wife I shall have?" he quipped, and led her on before she could answer. At the kitchen door he kissed her lingeringly, then gently pushed her inside and hurried off, saying only, "Good sleep, my love."

With a last look to ensure herself he had not been a mirage, Sarita trembled. Her heart longed to soar with happiness and yet shuddered, for she had chosen not to tell him of Mandel's treachery.

Chapter XVIII

The cheerful twittering of the birds aroused Sarita from a restless sleep at dawn. Pulling her pillow over her head, she tried to ignore their joyous celebration, but their chatter continued, much like the questions seething in her mind. Unable to sleep, she rose, intent on slamming the windows shut, until she saw Deborah's sleeping form. Dressing hurriedly, Sarita plaited and pinned her dark hair in place and went to the kitchen to begin the morning's breakfast, hoping that activity would ease the pain within her heart.

Why had Cris returned looking like a footpad and at so late an hour? Why had he cautioned her to be silent? These questions overrode her usual care, and pots and pans, spoons and dishes were rattled loudly as she went about her preparations.

"'Tis rubble you wish to be making?" Tessy's curt voice caused Sarita to start. "Miss, what be upon you?" She surveyed the jumble with questioning disgust. "Did ye not sleep at all, child?" The large woman's features became concerned upon seeing the young woman's distress. She ambled forward in a motherly fashion. "Why, ye ain't pining for that Lord Dunstan, are ye?"

"That is a ridiculous thought, Tessy. I'm only beginning breakfast for you," Sarita returned edgily.

"Thank you. I don't often have such help." The

older woman glanced over the disarray, hands on hips. Likely her mother was at it last night, she thought, and her look softened. "You just go back to bed, miss. I'll manage breakfast this morn. If everyone picks at their food as they did yesterday, there won't be much need of cooking." She patted Sarita's shoulder, edging her towards the door. "I wonder what that Mr. Sullivan will have to say for himself—if he comes back. You needn't look so wide-eyed, miss," she said, shaking her finger. "Many are saying he has reason and more to hope the earl meets with misfortune. The title be his if his lordship dies."

Colour drained from Sarita's features. She bolted from the kitchen, leaving Tessy sadly shaking her head.

Instinct directed her up the broad staircase towards her room. *What am I to do?* she asked herself. *I must know if this is true,* she thought wildly. Sarita's fists clenched as she thought of what Cris had asked her to do. I will go in Lady Brienne's place, she decided. But Cris had said there could be no questions. Do you not love him enough to trust him? her heart demanded.

"Why, Sarita, was that you in the kitchen?" the baroness asked, hurrying from her doorway to the perturbed young woman. "Why, child you are distressed. Have they found Lord Enoch?"

A shake of her head was all Sarita could manage.

"Your hands are like ice. Come in to my chamber." Lady Brienne guided Sarita forward.

The door was just closing behind her, and the young woman turned and grabbed the knob. "I must go," she blurted. "To help Tessy."

"That would not be wise," the baroness told her, placing her hand atop Sarita's. "The unusual disturbance I heard earlier will take some righting, and I doubt that Tessy will be in a fair mood doing it. Now, sit down." She took Sarita's hand from the door and gave her no time to object as she pushed her into a chair. Satisfied that she would remain seated, Lady Brienne rummaged beneath the feather beds, withdrew a silver flask, and poured a golden liquid into a glass. "Drink this," she commanded, putting the glass in Sarita's hands.

A large gulp of the apricot brandy momentarily relieved the young woman's turmoil; she gasped for breath.

"That's better." Lady Brienne sat down opposite her and was pleased to see colour returning to her features. "Now tell me what has upset you." She folded her arms and awaited the answer with a scrutinizing stare.

The effect of the brandy, or the challenge she read in this high-handed, white-haired old woman before her, firmed Sarita's resolve. Spirit replaced uncertainty in her eyes; her chin rose determinedly. "I don't believe it," she said adamantly.

"Neither do I," agreed the baroness crisply. "But could you tell me just what we don't believe?"

"They are saying Mr. Sullivan is responsible for Lord Enoch's disappearance. That he wishes the title for himself," tumbled from Sarita's lips.

"Of all the foolish gibberish!" Lady Brienne stiffened, her colour heightened. "Who has been spreading such a ridiculous rumour?"

Something in the baroness's tone caused Sarita to

squirm uncomfortably. "Tessy was only repeating what she heard others say."

"It's about time that woman met her come-up-pance. How dare she pass on such malicious gossip about my . . ."—the baroness's eye caught Sarita's inquiring gaze"—my nephew's secretary," she ended. "I will see it goes no further in this house, never fear." She reached across and patted Sarita's hand.

Grasping the baroness's hand, the younger woman asked, "If you loved a man and believed, truly believed, he was a good man, would you trust him completely? Even if it appeared . . . if circumstances seemed to say he was not?"

"If I loved him, yes," came the baroness's firm reply.

Peace flickered, then joy blazed in Sarita's eyes as she fully surrendered her heart. She leaned forward and whispered, "You are to meet Mr. Sullivan at the brook just beyond the garden as soon as you are able this morn. No one is to know about it."

"When did you receive this message?" asked Lady Brienne, her curiosity flaring.

Sarita shook her head, a blush brushing her cheeks. A wide smile came as she recalled Cris's words: "It would be interesting to hear your explanation."

"Come now, miss. What have you been up to?" Lady Brienne demanded.

"Nothing, my lady. Mr. Sullivan asked me to give you the message. I must think it strange of him not to come to see you himself."

"Ah ha! Waited until someone appeared in the kitchen this morn, did he? I suppose he heard about Henrietta's . . ." She halted in mid-sentence. "Of

course, he cannot dare to encounter her before . . .
I must go at once. If anyone should ask for me before
I return," she continued hurriedly, gathering her
bonnet and gloves, "tell them I felt like an early walk
and went towards Monsieur Mandel's." She winked.
"And tell Tessy I shall speak with her later."

"Can you manage it?" Lord Dunstan asked the
baroness as the two sat down on a fallen tree beside a
small stream.

"Henrietta was never easily governed. Your father
was one of the few to ever succeed," she cautioned.

"But can you do it?"

"If I have to tie her to her bed." Lady Brienne
snapped her fingers confidently.

"Nothing too desperate now. I hear Mother already
has endured a vase of water," Dunstan returned with
feigned horror.

"She was forewarned." Lady Brienne rose. "What
are Sullivan's chances of being alive?"

"They may believe he is of some use . . . as the
earl. But if they learn he is not . . ." He shrugged
forlornly. "We must find him soon."

"Do you believe Pergrine has him?"

"Feel you have me trapped at last, do you?" He
chuckled. "What else do you suspect?"

"It is more who than what at the moment. Pierre
Mandel is a wily young man. He knows much of what
occurs at Pergrine manor—more than his position
deems likely. He also wears the finest new French
silks, which the ladies of London would kill for, while
his father's clothing dates from before the revolution.
There is discord among those two, and not, I believe,

because Pierre smuggles brandy and cloth for his lordship. No, there is more. Much more to involve you to such a degree," she ended shrewdly. "Visiting your dear old aunts, eh?" she accused. "I think you seek Lord Pergrine and Pierre Mandel."

"The two are connected," Dunstan admitted slowly. "And now we have a third in sight. Lord Gerard arrives . . ."

"I know, but surely you do not suspect such a widely respected man as his lordship?"

"How do you know of Lord Gerard's coming?"

"Ah, through young Monsieur Mandel. There is to be a *grande célébration,* to use his words." She leaned forward conspiratorially. "According to Mandel, Lady Pergrine refused to let an opportunity to have so many extraordinary guests pass." She posed affectedly with a hand to her cheek. "Cannot say I blame the poor woman."

"Excellent," Dunstan smiled. "Who is included in your invitation? When is it to be held?"

"Why, everyone at the rectory has been invited. It is on Thursday next. But there is doubt about whether we should attend with Lord Enoch still missing."

"This may be the opportunity I need. You must convince Mother to go along with this matter and then persuade the Durhams to attend the ball. We need a signal . . . I know. Hang something white out of Lin's bedchamber window when Mother has surrendered to, ah, reason. The sooner I can appear here in public the better."

"But what of Lord Gerard?"

"He is an innocent dupe at this point, but he

handles some very important government and military papers."

"He is bringing them with him? But what would Pergrine do with them? Mandel?" she questioned. Understanding dawned. Her features twitched in anger. "Traitors."

"They will be dealt with," Dunstan assured her. "Now off to your confrontation with Mother." He rose and held out his hand to assist her.

"There is some one you should explain matters to," the baroness advised him as she accepted his hand. "Sarita has taken quite a buffeting, especially with all the gossip about Mr. Sullivan wanting the earl's title."

"Wanting the earl's title? But she does not believe . . . ?"

"Of course not. But then, the foolish girl loves you, scoundrel that you are. Such love deserves trust. Oh, I am not saying you must reveal all, but your activities bring to mind many suspicions . . . even to a loving aunt." She winked. "It would be easy to lay her fears to rest."

He squeezed her hand. "It shall be done. You know, my looks last eve would have frightened off a lass with less spirit." He smiled broadly.

"You saw Sarita during the night?"

"But didn't she . . . Oh," Dunstan teased, "I have evidently misjudged her abilities if she fobbed you off."

"Young man, you are incorrigible if not insulting." The baroness frowned. "But be warned. Do not underestimate Pergrine or Mandel. That could prove disastrous in this business of yours."

A loud crash echoed through the rectory, followed by upraised voices. Sarita and Deborah paused as they met in the corridor at the foot of the stairs.

"Do you think we should see what is happening?" Deborah asked, looking doubtfully up the stairs.

"Lady Brienne said she was not to be disturbed while she spoke with Lady Dunstan," Sarita answered.

"But that does not sound like a conversation. More like a battle. And why did the baroness insist that they remove to a bedchamber instead of using the solarium or sitting room? Do you think Lady Dunstan is all right?"

"They are sisters, Debs."

"That did not prevent Lady Dunstan's dousing. With all this strain . . ."

"Listen, it has become quiet. There is nothing to fret about. Do you want to come with me? Tessy has prepared a basket of food for the Strumms."

"No. I shall remain here. Father and Clem may return at any time with news."

"No more unnecessary fretting?"

"I promise I won't. I told Mother I would read to her this afternoon. You know how it eases her mind. Will you be gone long? Perhaps you should not go alone."

"I dislike asking any of the dowagers to go into the midday heat. If I see Ben or Josh, I'll ask them to walk with me," Sarita told her, marvelling at her sister's sudden concern.

A second outburst broke loose above them.

"I had best hurry to Mother," Deborah said. "She

will be upset by this. Give my greetings to Mrs. Strumm," she called back as she hastened up the staircase.

How considerate Debs has become, Sarita thought as she went to the kitchen to collect the basket of foodstuffs. *Reading to Mother, cautioning me. In the past these cares never entered her mind. And the change appears lasting,* her thoughts continued as she stepped out the kitchen door into the overly warm sunshine. The disappearance of the earl has achieved more than all of Father's lectures. She must love him as much as I care for Cris. "May the good Lord watch over us all," she breathed aloud as she walked through the woods. In a short time the Strumm cottage was before her.

"Miss Sarita be here! Miss Sarita be here!" the small children shouted, dashing to greet her.

"Now don't be mussin' miss's gown," Mrs. Strumm called out, coming to the door. "Pardon 'em, miss. They get so excited when ye come."

"I don't mind." Sarita toussled the hair of the little boy beside her. "As a matter of fact, I think there is a sweet cake for each of you . . . sent especially by Tessy." She grinned.

Four pairs of bright eyes looked longingly at the basket and followed on Sarita's heels as she entered the dark, dirt-floored hut. Sleeping mats for the children were neatly stacked beneath the only bed in the lone room. Poverty was apparent in the lack of furnishings. A single beef tallow candle stood on the worn table, the only source of evening light.

"God bless ye for yer kindness," Mrs. Strumm told

Sarita as the children rushed outside to eat their treats.

" 'Tis not our gift but that of Lord Dunstan."

"But ye be the one bringin' it, and ye have brought other gifts, even when there was naught for yer own house."

"I'm thankful we can help."

"Won't be needin' it much longer." The worn woman drew herself up proudly with a wan smile. "Me 'Enry be 'ome soon."

"We'll rejoice with you, Mrs. Strumm," Sarita said happily, thinking how the man had been caught poaching on Pergrine's land and sentenced to two years.

"But ye need a sip o' my wild basil tea. Ye be flushed 'n over 'eated."

"I must have hurried more than I meant to," she said, accepting the chipped cup of bitter brew. As horrid as the tea was, Sarita would never injure the woman's pride in being able to offer her something in return for the food. However, experience had taught her to gulp it quickly.

"Take a care, miss. Ye shouldn't be drinkin' it so quick-like. Would ye want more?"

"No, thank you, Mrs. Strumm. I must return right away, or Mother will fret." Sarita handed her the cup and picked up the empty basket.

"I 'ope they be findin' 'is lordship soon," the older woman said earnestly as they walked outside. "And take a care goin' 'ome."

"I will," Sarita assured her, smiling. With a wave of her hand she tripped lightly off into the woods. Thoughts of all the suffering Lord Pergrine had caused paced with her. If only the wrongs could be righted, she thought. Should we attend the ball? Does Lord Pergrine wish to change? And what of Cris? Had his talk with Lady Brienne precipitated the confrontation with Lady Dunstan? What would Cris have to do with an earl's mother? A soft burst of laughter escaped from inside the Hall. Such a beehive of questions, and no way to collect the answers. She had thought Debs was foolhardy. Who was the foolish one now? she asked herself, a soft smile coming to her lips.

Her steps halted abruptly as a man stepped from behind a tree to confront her. The happiness that filled her features upon thinking it was Cris faded as she recognized Pierre Mandel. "You should know better than to frighten people so," she snapped angrily.

"You did not look terrified when you first saw me, *ma chérie,*" Mandel said, trying to capture her hand.

"I wish you would not use those words," she told him firmly, not flinching from his piercing gaze.

"But you smiled so . . . Was there another you expected to see? That *bouffon,* Traunt?" He managed to catch her hand and squeezed it cruelly. With his other hand, Mandel wrenched the basket from her and threw it aside. Pulling her against him, he breathed, *"Ma chérie,* do you not know how long I have loved you?" His eyes seemed to strip her of her gown as she struggled. "You shall be no one's, only mine. Come away with me. As my wife, everything you desire shall be yours."

"Release me, Pierre," Sarita gritted, "and I shall forgive this . . ."

"Do you not see? The finest silks, the best wines, servants. All shall be yours."

Sarita ended his words with two hard kicks to his shins. Her heart chilled at the light in Mandel's eyes.

"You wish to make this *intéressant?* Such spirit. What a *mariage* we shall have." He forced her close, the hunger in his eyes burned her.

Twisting, she avoided his lips, shuddering as they brushed her cheek and neck. "I shall never marry you," she panted as she writhed in his hold.

"Think carefully, *ma chérie*. I shall have you . . . with or without *mariage*." Mandel's voice hardened. "Do not rouse my displeasure." He tightened his grip.

"You are hurting me," Sarita pleaded, deciding to change tactics. "How can you say that you love me?" She lowered her eyes as her struggling ended.

"You see, you need only speak." Pierre loosened his hold. "A kiss, *ma chérie*, for your future husband." His confidence sickened her.

"You must forgive me, please." She said coyly, despite her trembling, "but this is so unexpected, so sudden. I have . . . never . . . never kissed a man such as you," she breathed, keeping her eyes to the ground to prevent them from betraying her.

"Oh, *ma chérie*, I shall teach you all." Mandel's voice chilled her.

"But we must know one another better." Sarita forced herself to look at him, her face blazing red.

"How modest my bride is." Mandel brushed her cheek. "As you wish, *ma chérie*, but I am an impatient man."

"If I do not return soon, Mother will become worried." She tried to ease past him.

Mandel's hand closed on hers. He raised it to his lips. "And we mustn't make your mother fret. I shall come with you. It would be best to speak to your father *immédiatement*. We shall wed soon." Keeping her hand in his grasp, he led the way.

Sarita followed, her heart pounding at her narrow escape. If only the rectory would appear, she thought. Her heart leapt as she spied the bright yellow and green of the marchioness's and countess's parasols in the garden.

Mandel sauntered triumphantly up to them, Sarita's hand firmly held to his arm. "*Mesdames,* how lovely you are this beautiful day."

"You seem unusually gay, *monsieur,*" Lady Phillippa noted, fighting a surge of distaste at the young Frenchman's manner.

"Is something wrong, Sarita?" she questioned, seeing her wan looks.

"Nothing . . . now," she answered, reaching out her free hand.

Reluctantly, Mandel released his hold.

"You will leave at once," Sarita swung on him angrily.

Question, then anger flashed to his features.

"You are wrong, *monsieur,* to think I would marry a . . . a cur such as you."

Stepping forward threateningly, Mandel found two parasol points in his stomach.

"You have been asked to leave," Lady Phillippa said icily, applying pressure to hers.

"It is not wise to stay beyond one's welcome," Lady Imogene added.

A wine-red flush came to his features. Mandel clenched and unclenched his hands. "You shall regret this, *mademoiselle*," he spat, and turned and strode angrily away.

"He seemed such a nice young man," Lady Imogene tisked sadly as she lowered her parasol. "What a rather nasty look he had. Do you think we should have Ben and Josh keep watch in case he returns?"

"You had best remain indoors, Sarita, and have one of us with you whenever you do go out until Monsieur Mandel has had time to cool his feckless ardour," the marchioness cautioned. "A man scorned is no less dangerous than a spurned woman."

"What else shall happen?" the countess sighed heavily.

"Brienne and Henrietta could be reconciled. There hasn't been a sound for at least a half hour," Lady Phillippa noted hopefully.

"Perhaps Brienne realized the futility of her purpose and took action?" countered Lady Imogene.

"Purpose? Action?" Sarita questioned.

"You don't think she would . . . ?" The marchioness bit her lip.

"Of course not," the countess said, but her words were less than confident.

"Perhaps," Lady Phillippa began and paused. Without another word, the three women raised their skirts in unison and ran to the rectory.

Chapter XIX

Mandel stared at Lin Sullivan's battered face.

"Stubborn un, 'e be," the burly man beside him grunted. "Ain't said no more than 'e did the first time. 'Haps what ye 'eard tell o' 'im 'twerent true."

"I'll decide that. It could be I only need to find someone more capable than you to persuade him," Mandel sneered.

"I'd like ta see the likes o' ye or 'is lordship make the man talk," scoffed the other.

"The seed of a brain does lie in that noggin." The young Frenchman rubbed his chin. "When full darkness falls, take the earl to that deserted cottage near Pergrine Manor."

"Will 'is lordship 'prove o' 'avin' 'im so close like?"

"You take orders from me," Mandel snapped.

"But if 'e be found, it do point the finger at 'is lordship."

"Which should teach you something."

The burly figure stared stupidly, then began to chuckle. "A bit o' protection fer yerself, eh? Ye be the smart one."

"Then do as you're bid and keep watch out for Sullivan. Also put a watch out along the coast. I'm expecting *Le Blatte*. He must not be caught."

"Them's too stupid to catch the likes o' *Le Blatte*," jeered the other.

"And what of the brandy we lost?"

"T'was only a bad toss o' luck."

"If there is another such toss, 'twill be unfortunate . . . for you," warned Mandel and walked away. Certain no one was about, he slipped through the concealed opening of the cave and hurried through the woods towards Pergrine Manor. Twilight had fallen by the time he presented himself and asked to speak with his lordship.

While waiting in Pergrine's private study, Mandel eyed the richly finished Chippendale furniture and luxurious velvet drapery, this room being one of the few not stripped to pay for Pergrine's expensive habits. His hand caressed the polished desk top possessively.

"I told you not to come here," Lord Pergrine blustered angrily after the butler closed the door behind him. "It is too dangerous."

"What *risque* is there in discussing a greenhouse?" Mandel shrugged insolently.

"You fool. Don't you know Gerard is here? We must be careful. What do you want this time?"

"Lord Gerard's man, this Finley—is he willing to do as you said?"

"If the persuasion is high enough. Has the gold been delivered?"

"Do not fear, it shall be. When is the exchange to take place?"

"The night of the ball. At least there will be some advantage to Lady Pergrine's nonsense. Neither Finley nor I will be missed for some time. Will the boat be waiting if we choose to leave England?"

"As promised, my lord. And I shall be going with

you." Only Mandel's twitching lower lip revealed his anxiety over Pergrine's possible reaction to this news.

"But I thought you were to remain." Pergrine fidgeted nervously with his cravat.

"I will no longer be of use here. There is someone I wish to take to France." He picked up the letter opener on Pergrine's desk and ran his finger against the edge.

"Not Dunstan?" Pergrine asked fearfully.

"*Non,* he is to die. Mademoiselle Durham is to go with me." He poised a fingertip atop the point of the opener.

"One of the Durham chits, eh," laughed his lordship. "That will set old Durham's hackles."

"She will not be going willingly . . . at least not at first." Mandel's lips curled into a malicious smile.

"Not willing? You'd best leave her out of it then." Pergrine shook his head. "Only complicates matters. Makes it more dangerous for all of us. Finley won't take to it."

"She goes with us."

"No."

Mandel leaped to Pergrine's side, the letter opener against his lordship's heaving chest.

"Take your hands from me, Mandel. Without me you have no documents, no plans, no numbers."

Slowly, Mandel relaxed, lowered the knife, and sauntered back to the desk. "Lord Dunstan has been taken to the deserted cottage just north of this manor," he said, his back still to Pergrine.

Striding forward, his lordship spun him around. "You imbecile! Don't you realize the danger? Return him to the cave at once. Your men let him hear too much."

"Remove your hand, my lord." The Frenchman's cold, birdlike eyes raised fear in Pergrine. "Without me you do not have your gold. Lord Dunstan's nearness is to remind you of that."

"I've been true to my word," the other blustered. "You have always received what you wanted."

"And I shall continue to. It is no longer I who take the risks, my lord."

"I still think you should leave the Durham chit out of it. Think. She will be more easily missed than any of us," Pergrine insisted. His gaze wavered as Mandel remained unmoved. "And what of Dunstan?"

"As I said, he shall die," Mandel answered coldly.

"I must return to my guest." Pergrine fingered his cravat with a trembling hand. "Good eve, Mandel."

"My lord." Pierre bowed and watched his lordship scurry away like a rat on a well-waxed floor.

"Mr. Sullivan, you don't know how we've awaited your return," Reverend Durham greeted Dunstan as he stepped down from the phaeton before the rectory at dusk.

"I learned of Lord Enoch's disappearance when I halted at Runnet." Cris returned the firm handshake. "What has been done to find his lordship?"

"Clem Traunt and I have led searches for the past two days but to no avail."

"Could Traunt be summoned? I would like to speak with both of you about this matter."

"Of course. Mr. Caine will go for him at once, but I believe you should speak with Lady Dunstan," the reverend urged. "This has been a very difficult time for her. You *are* acquainted with Lady Dunstan?" Durham asked, sensing the other's reluctance.

"Rather better than is comfortable . . . at times," Dunstan said with a wry grin. "Will you take me to her ladyship? This had best be done at once."

"I am certain she does not hold you personally responsible for her son's disappearance," the rector sought to ease the young man's discomfiture as he led him towards the solarium.

"Is everyone inside?" Dunstan asked at the door.

Durham nodded.

The earl quietly opened the door and walked in. He felt seven pairs of eyes upon him as he halted before Lady Dunstan with a deep bow. From the corner of his eyes he saw Lady Brienne nod.

"You may straighten, Mr. Sullivan," Lady Dunstan told him haughtily.

"I sincerely regret my absence at the time of his lordship's disappearance and pledge to do all in my power to discover those responsible," said Cris.

"You do intend to find my son, then?"

"Every attempt is being made," Reverend Durham interposed quickly, sensing a brouhaha coming.

"Do you believe a ransom will be demanded?" she continued, ignoring the rector's words.

"I do not," the earl answered.

"That is fortunate. At this moment I would not pay a farthing for my son's return."

"Oh, Lady Dunstan," Deborah implored. "Surely you do not mean that."

Her ladyship's features softened as she took in Deborah's stricken look. "I do not, my dear. But"—her gaze returned to the earl—"my son does at times try me beyond the limits of maternal endurance."

"But it is not Lord Enoch's fault he was . . . kidnapped." Deborah's bottom lip quivered.

Exasperation spread over Lady Dunstan's features. She fanned herself with her kerchief, surrendering.

"My sister is curt because of her grief," Lady Brienne assured Deborah. "No one desires the safe return of the earl more than she."

"I am capable of speaking for myself, Brienne," Lady Dunstan interposed. She straightened her kerchief into a neat square, then looked at her son. "We are happy to see you safely returned, Mr. Sullivan," she said.

"Your journey here was pleasant, I trust," Dunstan said, sitting down on the sofa beside his mother, his eyes tossing a smiled greeting to Sarita.

"Abominable. It was horrid . . . as is any travel over country roads. And . . ."—a warning cough from the baroness caused her to pause. "But Mrs. Durham has been so kind since my arrival," she amended. "It quite makes up for the unpleasantness."

"I will see to the matter we discussed," Reverend Durham told Cris and excused himself.

Silence hung heavily for a few moments.

"Mr. Sullivan, could you perhaps advise us, knowing Lord Enoch as you do?" the baroness asked.

"I shall try," he managed with appropriate somberness.

"We have been invited to a ball at Pergrine Manor just two days hence . . ."

"And you question the appropriateness of attending it at such a time?" he finished for her. "With all respect," Dunstan took his mother's hand, "I can assure you that your son would wish you, all of you"—he glanced to the others—"to attend. Such action on your part," the earl added hastily, "could possibly cause the villains to drop their guard, to make an error that would lead us to his lordship."

"If that is true, I insist we all attend," Lady Dunstan replied. "Though it shall be difficult." She sighed theatrically.

"Until Lord Enoch is found, there can be no easy rest for any of us," Dunstan noted soberly, looking at no one.

"Sarita, I hoped I would find an opportunity to speak with you." Dunstan took her hand and drew her into the shadows of the Hall.

"Do you not fear the Ghost of Malvern?" she joked shakily as he took her in his arms.

"Lady Brienne has exorcised it," he stated with a chuckle. Gazing into her eyes, he became quite serious. "She has also told me of the gossip . . ."

"It does not matter." Sarita placed her fingertips on his lips to halt his words.

Kissing them lightly, he continued, "But it will in the days to come. And I mean for us to have many days together . . . a lifetime of days." Dunstan sighed heavily. "But first I must find Li . . . Lord Enoch."

"I am certain you shall."

"I wish I was as certain. You must recognize the possible danger. I am involved in trapping spies."

"Pierre?"

"How did you know?"

"Last night when I was returning to the rectory for the first time, I accidentally overheard him speaking with another man," Sarita answered reluctantly.

"What was said? It could be important."

"Something about a man, *Le Blatte,* that he wanted information before he sent more gold. Pierre told the man to tell *Le Blatte* he needed the gold for a . . . payment."

"Was there anything else?"

"Pierre also wanted a boat kept waiting on the shore, but the other man said he could promise nothing, that only by luck had brandy instead of gold been taken from them during a raid. Does it mean anything to you?" she asked.

"Yes, more than I have time to explain now. Beware of Mandel. He has no idea you heard this?"

"I am certain he did not," Sarita assured him.

"Pergrine is also involved in this. That is why we must attend the ball." He tilted her chin up. "There is a reason behind all this oddness."

"I know you shall explain when you are able." Complete trust warmed her words.

Dunstan's lips brushed hers, then held them fast as he crushed her against him. The danger about them was forgotten as their hearts twined in rapturous delight.

Chapter XX

"Before Traunt arrives, there is a personal matter I must speak with you about," the earl said to Reverend Durham after taking a seat before him in the library. "I am depending upon your confidentiality in this, for the entire matter cannot be cleared until . . . But I am getting ahead of myself." He lounged back, the earnestness in his eyes belying his indifferent pose. "First, a necessary confession. I am not Cris Sullivan, but Enoch Crispin Henry Edward Kennard, Earl of Dunstan. The man posing as myself, is, in truth, Lin Sullivan, my secretary." He paused.

"That explains much," Reverend Durham's deep voice noted calmly, no trace of surprise showing.

"The deception was a last thought, unplanned, a quirk on my part."

"Go on."

"I was sent here to learn how the French were getting detailed accounts of land and naval movements from someone in this area. I have been successful to a degree. I believe that Lin was taken either because he uncovered somthing of importance or because they have learned of my activities. If his true identity is revealed, his life will be forfeit." Dunstan was now leaning forward, all indifference gone.

"Did the dowagers know of this exchange of identities?"

"They discovered it only a short time ago. I had not seen them since I was a young boy. They have persuaded my mother to consent to the disguise."

"Persuaded?" Durham thought of the uproar he had heard earlier between the women. He nodded and flexed his jaw. "Do my daughters know of this?"

"No."

The rector's look hardened.

"I will tell Sarita everything as soon as Lin is safe. It is she I wish to speak of. I wish to ask for your daughter's hand in marriage."

"You believe she will accept you, even after learning of your deception?"

"I am hopeful she will understand the reason behind it. I love your daughter deeply, Reverend. I seldom have the opportunity to discern whether a woman cares for me or for my position and wealth. I have no doubt that it is I Sarita loves."

"Nor I," sighed Durham. "But is this not a cruel joke for Deborah?"

"Only if she wants the title alone. Lin is more a friend and companion to me. He has been my personal secretary, but that is at an end. He is a man of means and came with me on this journey as a personal favour. If your daughter loves him, it will not matter if he is simply Master Lin Sullivan, Esq."

A knock on the door ended their conversation.

"Enter," Reverend Durham called out, and Clem Traunt strode into the library. Dunstan rose and offered his hand.

The identity exchange was explained to Traunt, and the earl launched into a brief outline of his investigation and of Lord Pergrine's and Pierre Mandel's involvement.

"Then one of them has his lordship . . . I mean Mr. Sullivan?" Clem apologized.

"It would be best to continue as we have," said Dunstan. "I remain Sullivan until this is finished. But yes, I believe they do have Lin. And they are about to make a decisive move. The papers Finley carries are worth several thousand pounds to the French, but once he sells them, he cannot remain in England. Neither can Pergrine. Mandel may feel secure, though, because he has not taken an overt part in this maneuvering."

"I still find it difficult to believe that the man is actually a traitor," said Reverend Durham, shaking his head. "That he has the worst traits of the English peerage I readily agree. But to betray his country?"

"Pergrine is a desperate man, Reverend. Poor investments, mishandling of his holdings, and incessant gambling have all eaten at his funds and now there are none left. His lands will soon be taken from him by the duns. He is, in fact, a pauper."

"But even so, many men have lost more than he and not turned traitor."

"He has been lured by the promise of land, wealth, prestige, and power. Men have succumbed for far less," Dunstan finished. "My concern is to free Lin, gain proof against Mandel, Pergrine, and Finley, and prevent those documents from being handed over. Every cottager should be questioned. Someone must have seen something. My own men will continue scouring Pergrine's land.

"Your main task"—Dunstan's look included both

men—"will be to gather enough men to take care of the ruffians Pergrine keeps inside and outside of the manor. The night of the ball I shall be doing some exploring and want no interference. Besides, we must be certain that no one eludes us that night. Can you find enough willing men for the task?"

"Many's the man who's been wanting a go at those blackguards," Traunt answered, smiling.

"Good. Now for the details. As soon as it grows dark on Thursday night, I want you to begin working your way towards the manor," began Dunstan.

Thursday came with frightening suddenness, all attempts to find Lin fruitless. Last-minute details and alternative plans for the evening's rescue attempt kept Dunstan, Traunt, and Reverend Durham closeted in the library for most of the afternoon, while the chambers in the upper storey of the rectory were the scene of constant flurries of activity as the women readied themselves for the ball.

Petticoats were pressed, re-starched and pressed again. Gowns were chosen, discarded, and re-chosen as the dowagers struggled with the Misses Durham's toilettes as well as their own.

Deborah reluctantly took part, consenting only when reminded that going to the ball would aid Lord Enoch. Her pleasure came from Sarita's excitement. Could this sudden interest in gowns, ribbons, and furbelows be caused by Mr. Sullivan?" she teased.

"Does it show so terribly?" Sarita sighed as she turned before the looking glass, inspecting the last-minute alterations of her gown.

"The pair of you could light a room," Deborah

laughed. "Do you think he will speak to Father soon?"

A wave of sadness darkened the other's features, but she returned lightly, "He has been speaking with Father all day."

"You know what I mean." Deborah grimaced at her. "He is going to, isn't he?"

"Cris has said we shall wed . . . and I have not disagreed, but how can I, Debs, with Mother as she is? No, I shall take what happiness I can for now."

" 'Tis cruel you are being, Sarry—far crueller than I would have ever believed. How can you play with Mr. Sullivan's affections with so little concern? 'Tis plain to everyone how much he cares for you," Deborah challenged.

"I do love him, Debs, but my duty is to Father and Mother," she protested weakly.

"Rubbish and balderdash." Deborah laughed and rose. "Now I sound like you." She embraced her sister. "You are being the foolish one. Mother is weak because we allow . . . encourage her to be. Besides, they shall still have me."

"No." Sarita gripped her sister's arm. "Cris shall find your Enoch."

"Perhaps," Deborah sighed sadly, then forced a bright smile. "But for this eve we must dress you to outshine everyone at the ball. Mr. Sullivan will know he has found the most beautiful woman in the kingdom."

Sarita burst into laughter at her sister's posturing. "That is like thinking Enoch is a secretary and Cris an earl," she giggled.

"Then you would have to endure Lady Dunstan."

Deborah also giggled, and they both broke into laughter. But their emotions were taut and tears quickly threatened.

"Her ladyship can be very kind," Sarita defended the earl's mother, daubing at the corner of her eyes. "She is even likeable when she forgets herself."

"Oh, Sarry." The two hugged once more. "I don't care how Lady Dunstan is or whether or not Enoch is an earl. I only care that he is safe."

"I know Debs, I know." The two held each other tightly.

Late Thursday afternoon, a heavy knock on the library door brought the three heads peering over a drawing of the Pergrine estate up with a start. The drawing was quickly rolled and laid upon the floor behind the desk.

"Yes?" Reverend Durham called.

Davy Caine stuck his head in warily. "There be a fellow callin' himself Jervy wantin' to see Mr. Sullivan."

"Where is the man?" The earl rose hastily.

"I didn't like his looks. Ben and Josh are watchin' him in the stable."

A bark of laughter escaped Dunstan. "That'll be Jervy all right. Bring him here, quickly," he ordered.

A nod from Reverend Durham sent Caine on his way.

The little man, his garb indistinguishable beneath a layer of dust and grime, danced into the library. He went straight to Dunstan. "We've found him, m'lord."

Dunstan grabbed the man's shoulders. "Alive?"

"Aye, m'lord. A little worse for the beatin's he's been gettin', methinks, but breathin' strong." The man's eyes twinkled.

"Thank God," breathed the earl, dropping his hands. "Where is he? No, wait. Davey, not a word of this to anyone. Go back to the stables and ready one of the best mounts there."

"Gladly, milord." He bowed with a wide grin, then left hurriedly, closing the door carefully as he went.

"Now, Jervy, where is Lin? Are there many guards?"

"One question at a time, m'lord." Jervy waved a begrimed hand. Seeing the map Reverend Durham was unrolling, he pounced on it. "There be the spot . . . a cottage."

"That building hasn't been used for near a year," Traunt noted. "Not since Pergrine threw the renter in gaol and tossed the poor wife and wee ones out."

"I thought this had been checked earlier," the earl questioned sharply.

" 'Twere, m'lord," Jervy answered. "He's only been there two . . . three days at most."

"How did you find him?" Reverend Durham asked.

"Took a poacher from a pair of Pergrine's men last eve." Jervy flashed a row of crooked teeth. "When we'd convinced him we were friends, he told us 'bout a queer bunch scuttlin' back and forth. Said last time he saw them they were carryin' a big bundle which looked suspiciously like a body. Led us right to 'em, he did. Three men there most times," he added, looking to Dunstan.

"Can we handle that?" Dunstan flicked Clem's shoulder.

"Aye," the other grinned.

"What about the men?" the earl questioned Jervy.

"Left two watchin' the cottage. The rest are prowlin' the shoreline, keeping watch for *Le Blatte*."

"I'm going with you," Reverend Durham told them.

"No." The earl shook his head. "You have to stay here, to escort the women should we be delayed," Dunstan told him. "Tell them nothing. We will meet you at Pergrine's." He threw his words over his shoulder as he followed Jervy and Traunt from the library.

The sun dimly shadowed the forest as it set for the night. Dunstan and his two companions had joined the two men already watching the cottage in which Lin was being held. Waiting for full darkness, they saw candlelight flicker to life inside.

"Someone's comin'," Jervy whispered. "A tall, thin man. Mandel."

"Do we take him now?" Clem whispered.

"No, I want him at Pergrine's," Dunstan whispered.

Inside the cottage, the young Frenchman taunted Lin. "My lord," he bowed, "you do not seem well. The gout, perhaps?"

"Aye, the gout," the three men standing behind Mandel jeered.

"I am sorry it is going to prevent you from attending Lord Pergrine's ball. In fact,"—Mandel smiled apologetically—"it is going to prove quite fatal to you."

Lin remained quiet, staring at Mandel contemptu-

216

ously while he inwardly cursed the cloth that bound his hands and gagged his mouth.

"Console yourself, my lord, with the thought that Miss Durham shall be mine, not yours as those meddling aunts of yours intended." Mandel's maliciousness ripened as he imagined the dowagers' reaction upon learning he had swept Sarita away with him. "You English lords are such fools," he spat derisively. "Take him to our rendezvous. The sea is to claim another. Weight him well with his English rocks," he laughed. "Then wait for me. This night we return to France," he told his men. "Keep a keen watch. Get him to his feet now."

From the underbrush Dunstan and Traunt saw the cottage suddenly darken. Mandel and his men came out, dragging Lin with them.

"Hold fast," the earl whispered as Jervy began to rise. They watched the conference and remained still as the Frenchman headed towards Pergrine Manor, and his men forced a staggering Lin in the opposite direction. Calculating quickly, Dunstan said, "We must alter our plans. Jervy, you take the men and follow them. When they've reached their destination, free Lin and scuttle back to the manor. Clem, you gather your men and surround Pergrine's. Do as we planned there. I'll come after I've dressed."

Jervy shook his head. "I don't like it, m'lord. Why not take him from them now?"

"Because you know how long you could search those coves and points before the boat would be found. They won't harm Lin getting him there. Be off with you before you lose sight of them," Dunstan ordered. "Take your horses with you. You may have need of them."

With a curt nod, Jervy and the other two men hurried after Mandel's men. Dunstan and Traunt lost no time in reaching and mounting their hidden horses.

"Remember, pick off Pergrine's bullies by one's or two's. Don't do anything that will raise alarm. Your purpose is to stop anyone from escaping. Good luck."

"The same with you," Clem saluted, and the two spurred away.

Chapter XXI

In the lowering evening light, a disappointed, sombre group stood uneasily about the steps and drive before the rectory.

"I think it best we go," Lady Brienne announced, gathering her skirts and approaching one of the two coaches awaiting them.

"I agree," Reverend Durham told the others. "Mr. Sullivan told me he would join us at the ball if he was late in returning."

"Are you certain he did not say where he was going?" Lady Dunstan asked, reluctantly following the baroness to the first coach.

The rector shook his head as he helped his wife into the second coach. "Come, Sarita, Deborah. We are late as it is."

"You don't think any harm has come to him, do you, Father?" Sarita asked as he assisted her into the coach.

"No, little princess." He gave her hand a reassuring squeeze. "He will return to you." The warmth of her smile twisted his heart. Would she understand the deception as readily as Dunstan believed?

The brief journey to Pergrine Manor was made in silence in the rector's coach, but with less tranquility in the dowagers'.

"Ladies," the baroness's quiet, firm voice silenced

the cacophony. "If we are to be of aid to Enoch
—Crispin,"—she conceded to Henrietta's scowl— "we
must be in harmony. Let us each select a task for the
evening so that we do not hinder more than help."

"For once we are in agreement," Lady Henrietta
answered, peering down her sharp nose.

"I propose that you"—Lady Brienne nodded to
Lady Imogene and the marchioness—"stay close to
Sarita and Deborah. Especially if that young Mr.
Mandel is present.

"You and I, Henrietta, shall maintain a watch on
Lord Pergrine and Lord Gerard's man."

"But how shall you know them?" Lady Imogene
brushed back a lock from her round face.

"When we are announced, I will simply ask the
footman to point him out," Lady Brienne answered.

"How can we be certain he is the one handing the
papers over?" asked Lady Phillippa.

"Crispin said Lord Gerard was merely a dupe. A
trusted secretary is the only one who would have
ready access to his papers."

"But where is Crispin?" Lady Dunstan asked worriedly.

"Mr. Caine told me he went with Mr. Traunt and
another man," began Lady Phillippa.

"Why didn't you tell me this before we left?" Lady
Henrietta snapped. "Driver," she called out, tapping
on the coach's roof.

"I instructed Mr. Caine to halt only on *my* command," the baroness told her. "Crispin is in the act of
or has already rescued Mr. Sullivan by this time. He
will appear at the ball, be certain of that."

"I had so hoped he would see Sarita as she came down the staircase," Lady Phillippa sighed.

"Who would have thought Mrs. Durham had such exquisite gowns as a young woman. The lilac silver tissue is perfect on Sarita," the countess noted.

"Sarita was . . . becoming," Lady Dunstan felt compelled to add.

"Beautiful," the baroness corrected. "Just the daughter-in-law for you, Henrietta. She won't brook your fustian. You will enjoy her."

" 'Tis apparent Crispin adores her and she him, but what will happen when she learns that he has been deceiving her? I fear even his title will not lessen Miss Durham's indignation." Lady Henrietta frowned worriedly.

"Never fear. Sarita is a sensible young woman, and if she hasn't enough sense . . . why then, we shall give her a suitable amount," stated Lady Brienne with a wink. "Our concern for this night is our individual quarries. Do not lose sight of yours at any time," she emphatically admonished the three ladies, tapping the coach's floor with the gold-knobbed cane she had chosen to use that evening.

With growing timidity, Sarita and Deborah followed their parents up the grand marble staircase which was wreathed with greenery and flowers for the evening. They sensed rather than heard their names being announced as they paused at the entrance of the huge upper gallery. The Pergrine ancestors, properly dusted, gazed blankly upon the dancers below them amid brilliant candelabras and bouquets.

A few guests glanced up casually at the mention of

Reverend Durham's family. Their eyes widened in pleasant surprise as they beheld the daughters.

Always considered fair because of her light hair, Deborah was enchanting in the stylish jade-green silk Lady Phillippa had loaned her. The pallour of her features caused by days of worry enhanced her glow of fragility. More surprising was Sarita's dark beauty, for she had long roamed the countryside in frayed gowns and mismatched aprons and bonnets. The lilac silver tissue gown, worn by her mother as a young lady in the '70s, had been stripped of the rows of ruching about the hem, skirt, and bodice. The wide lace trim had been removed from the full, puffed sleeves and the square neckline, and the silver tissue half overskirt had been eliminated from the waist. With these furbelows gone, it looked like a Grecian gown of current style, the raised waistline complementing Sarita's petiteness, the sheer material flattering her softly curved form. With her dark locks pulled back, twisted into a knot and pinned at center back, a gentle roll of hair framed her features, while the lilac ruche flowers about the knot glistened against the smooth black sheen of her hair. The quiet elegance of manner with which she carried herself transformed the country rector's daughter into a woman easily taken for one of the *haut ton*.

"Miss Durham—Sarita—will make an excellent countess," Lady Henrietta whispered to the baroness a short time later. "See how she dances, as if born to it." She glanced about nervously. "I do wish Crispin would come. I have the most dreadful feeling something has . . ."

"There is Mr. Finley," Lady Brienne interrupted. "Go after him. I must see to Lord Pergrine."

"Why, Baroness Mickle." Pierre Mandel bowed before her just as Lady Brienne began to step away.

Though he was perfectly attired for the occasion in form-fitting white knee breeches, an evening jacket of black with a white silk cravat at his neck, and a white with black striped waistcoat complementing it, she felt a surge of distaste for the man.

"Would you honour me with this dance?" he asked smoothly, taking her gloved hand and brushing it with a kiss. "I thank you for remaining true to your word," Pierre added, nodding towards Sarita, who was surrounded by admirers.

"I always do, *monsieur*," Lady Brienne clipped.

"The dance?"

Seeing Lord Pergrine lead Lady Imogene to the assembling dancers, the baroness nodded her consent. At the end of the set, Mandel bowed once again. "It has been most *plaisant*." His voice belied his eyes.

Cold fear came to Lady Brienne as she saw him look at Sarita. The malicious smile that curved his lips as he sauntered away rang as clearly as any spoken threat. The baroness fanned herself rapidly, her unease growing even when Mandel walked past Sarita with a wordless nod. She relaxed slightly when she saw the countess, in her rose-coloured gown, returning to the young woman's side. With a quick glance she noted a cool Henrietta in dogged conversation with a perspiring Mr. Finley. A further check showed Lady Phillippa visiting with Lady Pergrine, her arm wrapped through Deborah's. The baroness's eye scanned the crowded gallery hoping to catch sight of her nephew, for the hour was growing late and she knew Pergrine would conclude his dealings with Finley long before the ball ended.

At the end of the next country set, the orchestra took a brief pause, and Lady Brienne hastened to position herself near Lord Pergrine. Overhearing him excuse himself to a guest, she stuck out her cane as he passed, nearly tripping him. "How clumsy of me," she piped an apology. "Have you injured yourself, my lord? I could never forgive myself if you have. Truly, how utterly abominable of me. Do forgive me," she babbled, taking hold of his arm.

"It is nothing, Lady Bawden." He forced a smile to his lips. "I hope you are enjoying yourself. Let me get you a glass of champagne." Pergrine began edging away, only to find the baroness's hand glued to his arm.

"This is such a lovely ball," she simpered, "but I have not been able to visit with Lord Gerard. He is an old and dear friend, you know. Would you mind terribly helping me find him?" She fanned herself delicately.

"But . . ."

"I just knew you would." Lady Brienne lurched the surprised man forward, making certain she was going in the opposite direction from that taken by Lord Gerard when he had walked past her a short time before.

Lord Pergrine became increasingly nervous as the time passed. He was frantic to escape the baroness when the orchestra struck up the strains of an allemande.

Casting about for Finley and Mandel, Lady Brienne's eye caught sight of a broad-shouldered man at the entrance of the gallery. "At last," she murmured.

"What, my lady?" Pergrine followed her gaze. "Sullivan, isn't it?"

She nodded as she took in her nephew's handsome figure.

The local ladies had also noticed Mr. Sullivan's manly cut. His superfine cutaway jacket of deepest violet lay smoothly across his shoulders, little disguising their brawn. His jabot and cravat were of palest violet. Pale cream knee breeches and hose clung to his muscular calves and thighs. A sigh escaped the younger women when he nonchalantly brushed a hand slowly through his dark curls as he surveyed the crush.

Sarita saw all of this as if through a haze. He could have been attired in rags, and she still would have seen him as the handsomest man present. Her heart thumped wildly as he came through the throng and halted before her with a gracious bow. His eyes twinkling mischievously, Dunstan held out his hand. "May we dance, Miss Durham?"

"As you wish." She copied his manner, bobbing a quick curtsy.

"You are the most beautiful woman in all of England," he breathed in her ear, bending near as they took their places in the set. The dance began, preventing Sarita from replying, but her gaze upon him said all she could have spoken.

Mandel cursed as he watched them. Then he slipped from the gallery through a passage used by the servants.

Seeing the door close behind him, Lady Brienne

225

reached to take hold of Lord Pergrine and found him gone. "Horsefeathers and damnation!" she exclaimed angrily.

"Pardon, my lady?" A hawk-nosed woman peered at her through tinted spectacles.

"Be damned," the baroness snapped and stalked off, leaving the shocked woman with gossip for weeks to come. It took her some time to find any of her sisters, but finally she nabbed Lady Phillippa, and the two circled the gallery, hoping to see Lord Pergrine.

"Did you see Lord Pergrine leave?" Lady Brienne asked the countess as they joined her.

"No, I have been staying near Deborah, and a difficult task that is with the crush about her," Lady Imogene said, a wide smile on her round face. It dimmed at the others' stern looks.

"Pergrine and Mandel are gone," snapped Lady Brienne. "Where is Henrietta?"

"She and Mr. Finley left the gallery before the orchestra paused," the countess told them. "That was some time ago. Do you think . . . ?"

"I think they have escaped us. As soon as this country set ends, get Crispin. Tell him they are gone. It's a bloody poor time for him to be mooning over Sarita." She shook her head angrily.

" 'Tis only their second dance," the marchioness excused him.

The baroness rolled her eyes at these words and took Lady Phillippa in tow. Together they sauntered to the entry. She glanced back to see if anyone was watching, then said, "Come along," and took the steps two at a time.

* * *

"What do you mean, escaped you?" Dunstan drew Lady Imogene aside. "Why were you watching them in the first place? Don't you realize the danger? Where is the baroness now?" His questions beleaguered the hapless countess.

"She and Phillippa went to find Henrietta," she managed weakly before his wrath.

"Oh, Lord. Stay here. I do not need a fourth body to trip over," he snapped and striding towards the entrance, brushed past Sarita wordlessly.

"What did you tell him?" Sarita asked, joining Lady Imogene.

"He said he didn't need a fourth to trip over." The countess's lips hardened into a thin line. "He did not see us handle the French gendarmes in 'eighty-three when we were in France. Well, Brienne and Philly are not going to have all the fun, nor get all the credit." She stamped her foot. "Deborah, you had best return to your mother and stay close to her." Lady Imogene suddenly recalled the young woman behind her. "Young man," the countess commandeered a gentleman walking past. "Take Miss Durham to her mother," she ordered, placing Deborah's hand upon his arm. Pleased with herself at this maneuver, she was ready to proceed. "Aren't you coming?" She looked back when Sarita didn't follow.

"I suppose I shall." Sarita tossed aside her hesitation caused by Cris's stern expression, and hurried after the short, waddling figure.

"Do you know where you are going?" Lady Phillippa asked uneasily as the two dowagers wended their way through a maze of corridors and rooms.

227

"I saw a drawing of this manor in Reverend Durham's library," Lady Brienne answered.

"You went through his papers?"

"And the private chambers are in the wing just ahead," the baroness continued, ignoring her sister's words.

"Aren't you going to find Henrietta first?"

"Knowing Henrietta, she will have gone beyond caution and . . . Wait. Do you hear that?"

"What?" the marchioness asked, then clasped her hand to her heart as she heard the muffled thud, thump, thud. "Where is it coming from?" she whispered.

Lady Brienne shook her head. "This direction." She stepped back a few paces along the way they had come.

The thump, thud, thud, thump sounded louder.

"Check that room." The baroness opened a door on her side of the corridor and pointed to the one next to it.

"But it is dark in there."

"Take a candle," Lady Brienne said, wrenching one from a wall sconce.

"But I can't reach one."

"Really, Philly. Follow me," she snapped irritably. "It will take twice the time, but you needn't have an apoplexy. No, it didn't come from in here." She surveyed the empty chamber with some surprise. "How odd that there is no furniture," she muttered as she crossed the corridor to the chamber opposite.

Lady Phillippa stayed tightly on her heels.

The candle's weak flame showed only a large

wardrobe in the room. Thump, k-thump, came from it.

Gasping, the marchioness turned to flee but found that Lady Brienne had a firm hold on her skirts.

"You open the door, and I'll hit whatever . . . or whomever is in it," the baroness whispered, nodding at her cane.

Reluctantly, Lady Phillippa edged toward the wardrobe. Casting a pleading look over her shoulder, she received only a contemptuous scowl. With a pounding heart, she reached for the latch, jumping back when something shook the door from the inside. "I'm doing it, I'm doing it," she whispered, prodded by her sister's cane. Using both hands, she pried the latch open.

The doors flew apart and a ghoulish white mound tumbled to the floor, evoking a piercing scream from Lady Phillippa. "W . . . w . . . what do you think it is?" She clung to the baroness's arm.

"Those look bloody well like Henrietta's pumps." Lady Brienne took in the red-heeled black shoes sticking out from beneath the sheet. "Unfasten the rope," she ordered, holding the candle over the kicking figure.

The rope undone, Lady Henrietta tossed the sheet from her head. "Whatever took you so long?" she demanded, struggling to rise. She kicked the sheet from her feet. "I heard whoever clapped that over me say he had the gold ready."

"We must hurry then. They may have already exchanged it for the documents," the baroness told her, hurrying to the door.

* * *

At the same moment, in a different part of the manor, Lady Imogene and Sarita halted before a towering man in footman's garb. "Guests are not allowed in his lordship's private apartments," the man said threateningly.

"We must have taken a wrong turn," the countess twittered. "We merely wanted to freshen up a bit. Come along, Sarita, dear." She led the way back down the corridor, ducking into the first doorway out of his sight.

"What can we do?" Sarita asked. "We cannot get past that guard."

"There must be a way. Brienne did it." She glanced about. "Look, this door is not latched." Lady Imogene followed as it quietly swung open.

The dim light of the hall was reflected in four large windows, one of which was open.

"You don't mean to go out it," Sarita protested as the countess stuck her head out the window and examined the ground below.

"Mr. Sullivan may need our help."

"But in these gowns?" Sarita bemoaned the difficulty.

"Quiet, I hear steps."

Running feet in the corridor raced past the room. Voices were raised where the guard stood. The sound of a struggle broke out, then silence prevailed once more.

"I'll go first," Sarita said, in spite of the lump of fear in her throat. Sitting on the ledge, she swung her feet over it and jumped lightly to the ground just three feet below.

Getting Lady Imogene's ample form through the

window proved more difficult, but after many false starts, this feat was accomplished as well.

"Now what?" Sarita whispered.

"If I were Brienne, I would head towards that light in the wing ahead." Lady Imogene waddled through the shrubbery, waving for Sarita to follow.

In the corridor outside the chamber they had just left, Dunstan swiftly dragged the unconscious footman into the nearest room. Stripping him of his jacket and breeches, he tied the man's hands and feet. After exchanging these garments for his own, he edged from the room, pulling the door shut behind him, the man's pistol in his other hand. With the positions of both Finley's and Pergrine's chambers in mind, he chose the latter's and raced forward. Slowing his steps as he neared it, Dunstan stole to the door, hoping to hear if they had his aunts and to learn their intent towards the women.

Outside the manor, Lady Imogene had reached a row of shrubbery less than twenty feet from the lamp-lit window. "Sarita," she whispered. "Sarita?" She turned when no answer came.

A huge shadow loomed over the countess. A strong hand shut over her face. Recovering from her initial shock, Lady Imogene struggled, clamping her teeth over a salty finger as the man softly swore. Stars flashed, consciousness faded, and she sank to the ground.

Meanwhile, Lady Henrietta, the marchioness, and Lady Brienne had reached the corridor upon which

Pergrine's chambers opened. Spying a man, garbed as one of Pergrine's footmen with a pistol in his hand, standing at the door, they paused, then retreated.

"We'll never get past him," Henrietta fretted.

"Let's keep watch. He may be called into the room," the baroness told them.

"What good will that do?" Lady Phillippa asked.

"Don't ask so many questions. Come along," Lady Brienne snapped in a whisper, stealing back to the corner to watch.

Chapter XXII

"There is the boat," Jervy whispered to the two men with him. "Looks like we best lose no time."

On the rocky point below, the three men had thrown Lin roughly to the floor of the half-hidden boat and were debating the size and number of anchors needed to ensure that his body would not drift to shore.

While they argued, Jervy and his companion crept down the slope. Pointing out a man for each with his drawn pistol, Jervy rose from behind the concealing boulders. "That be as far as ye'll go this night," his voice rang out.

Cursing, Mandel's men clamoured over the rocks, trying to escape. A shot rang out, and the one farthest from Jervy fell. The other two halted, surrendering. "Look to 'em," he ordered his men and stuck his pistol in his waistband. Scrambling over the rocks, he set the shielded lantern the three had brought with them beside the boat and clambered into it. Slashes of his knife severed the rope binding Lin's hands and feet. With a strength belied by his size, he shouldered Sullivan, carried him to a small sandbar at the end of the point, and gently laid him down.

"Here, here, Mr. Sullivan." Jervy daubed Lin's bruised face with a seawater-soaked kerchief. "Ye be among friends." He fended off a weak blow thrown by the barely conscious man. "That's it, me lad," Jervy said cheerfully, helping him sit up.

"Where . . . where am I?"

"As near death's door as yer likely to get fer many a year to come," the other chuckled. " 'Tis the Channel," he added.

"Then Mandel's been caught." Relief flowed through Lin's aching body.

"Like as not he has. His lordship's after him at Pergrine's."

"You don't know for certain?"

"Nay, his lordship sent us after you. He 'n that Traunt fellow were headed to Pergrine's last I saw 'em. Don't fret. He'll handle Mandel."

"But does he know the man intends to kidnap Deborah, Miss Durham?" Lin grabbed hold of Jervy's blouse.

"Won't matter what he intended if he's already caught, 'n that's a surety," the little man answered, attempting to calm him.

"We've got to get them. Right away," Lin insisted, trying to rise. His legs, stiff from lack of exercise and being bound, buckled.

"Best we get ye to Durham's. Ye look a sight." Jervy shook his head.

"I'm going to Pergrine's if I have to crawl," Lin grated.

"All right, Mr. Sullivan. Seein' as how yer game fer it." He pulled him to his feet and supported him as they staggered over the rocks. "One of ye stay here, out of sight. Treat them louts proper-like," he yelled. "The other go find the rest of the men."

Back at the horses, Lin pulled himself into the

saddle with Jervy's help. "Lead on, as fast as you dare," he ordered, grabbing hold of the saddle to steady himself. He gritted his teeth against the pain as Jervy did exactly that.

The conversation beyond Pergrine's door had become heated. Dunstan strained to hear the muffled words.

"Mandel . . . made . . . fool . . . Has papers now," the earl made out. "Those dowagers . . . Dunstan . . . kill," came next, and he decided it was time to act. Slowly he pushed the door open, slipping in quietly.

Pergrine spied him and lunged for a pistol on the table beside him. Finley threw himself against the earl, knocking him against the door, stunning Dunstan and causing his pistol to discharge into the air.

"It's Dunstan," Finley gasped. "I thought Mandel had him."

"That's not the earl. It's his man, Sullivan," Pergrine sneered.

"I've spoken with Dunstan when he's called on Lord Gerard. This is the earl, and if he's onto this, our wick is snuffed. What are we going to do?" Finley asked, frantic with fear.

"There is a boat waiting on the coast not far from here."

"Not if Mandel promised it." Finley rushed to the window. Shadows were swarming on the grounds outside. "Dunstan has men surrounding the manor. We're trapped."

"Not I," Pergrine spat. "He goes with us."

"We can't carry him and the gold."

"The gold has been sent ahead. If Mandel only has one boat, it will be mine. Let's tie his hands." He motioned to the earl. "Hurry."

Together they bound Dunstan's hands behind him and heaved him to his feet. "Blow out the lamp, and snuff the candles," Pergrine ordered.

Outside, Clem Traunt and his men lost their smiles as the chamber darkened. "Stretch out, men," he ordered. "Keep a keen watch." Gathering ten men, he led the way around the wing, stationing a few at the likely exits but keeping three with him as he entered the manor through a window.

"Back, back," the baroness whispered urgently in the hall as she heard Pergrine come towards the door.

"Let's go," they heard Pergrine order and peeked around the corner to see him and Finley supporting a footman.

"That's not a footman, it's Crispin!" Lady Henrietta poked her sister. "We can't let them take him."

"Shh. They'll hear you, and my cane is no match for that pistol. Let's try to follow. Stop treading on my heels," she said over her shoulder as she was trod on by both.

"Where do you suppose they're going?" Lady Phillippa asked.

"There must be an exit . . ."

"Think, Brienne, think," Lady Dunstan implored as they slunk along.

The baroness halted. "It could work . . . but it could also be the death of one of us."

"What is your plan? I'll do anything."

"Anything to save Crispin," Lady Phillippa added to Henrietta's entreaty.

"Here is what we must do," Lady Brienne whispered hurriedly. "Do you understand?" she ended seconds later. "Surprise is our only hope. Remember: be extremely quiet till they see us." Firmly gripping the end of her cane, the baroness slipped her pumps from her feet; her sisters did likewise.

Tiptoeing, they hastened forward, dodging from doorway to doorway as they slowly drew near their quarry.

Suddenly Pergrine spun around. Banshee howls and screams came from the three elderly women as they flew at him, arms waving, skirts flying. Unnerved momentarily, his pistol wavered before taking aim at Dunstan's head, allowing just enough time for Lady Brienne to swing her cane with all her might.

Wood met flesh with bonebreaking force. The pistol fell, unfired, as Pergrine yelped with pain.

Finley released his hold of the earl and dashed down the corridor as the dowagers descended upon him.

"After him!" the baroness commanded, her foot stepping upon Pergrine's good hand as he scrambled after his pistol.

Tripping in his frenetic rush, Finley found himself belted and battered as the marchioness and Lady Henrietta fell upon him with a fury.

Moments later Clem Traunt appeared. For a moment he considered leaving the traitor to the mercies of the women, but concern for Dunstan outweighed that wish. "Ladies, my ladies." He caught the marchioness's arm. "Enough. Let him live for the hangman."

Drawing back as Traunt hauled Finley to his feet, Lady Henrietta and Lady Phillippa straightened themselves haughtily, smoothing their gowns and patting their ruined coifs.

"You could have managed to come a bit sooner, Mr. Traunt," Lady Brienne's accusing voice rang in his ear.

"You've got Pergrine," Clem gasped, seeing his lordship huddled against the wall, his broken arm cradled in his lap while the baroness poised threateningly over him with her cane. "That's bloody well done," he congratulated her as he pushed Finley into the arms of his men. "Now to find Lord Dunstan."

"That is done." The earl shook his head to clear it as he struggled to sit up, his hands still bound behind him.

Rushing to him, Clem quickly untied the cord. "Bloody good show, my lord."

" 'Twas the dowagers." He smiled and rubbed his sore head. "You've got Mandel, then?"

"I thought he was still in the manor. Didn't see anyone leave," Traunt answered blankly.

"He's made a fool of you as well as me," Pergrine spat. "You'll never get him now."

"At least everyone is safe." Dunstan looked at the three sisters, his mother and Lady Brienne arm in arm.

The baroness nodded. "Sarita's safe with Lady Imogene, but what of Mr. Sullivan?"

"Lin should be free by now. I sent my men after him," he said, pulling Pergrine to his feet. "You are

238

fortunate he was not badly harmed. Take them to the high-sheriff," he told Clem.

"But he's at the ball," Traunt answered.

No need to spoil your celebration." The earl cocked his head at Pergrine. "I recall you have a very sound gaol. Secure them and any men you've taken. Then come join us, Mr. Traunt."

"Gladly, m'lord." He signaled his men to escort the two traitors down the corridor.

"And you, my ladies"—Dunstan bowed with a flourish—"will allow me to return you to the ball."

The three dipped into deep curtsies and broke out laughing.

"I just hate to think what Imogene will say when she hears what she has missed," Lady Phillippa laughed, taking the earl's arm.

"Oh, lud." The baroness rolled her eyes at the thought. "Don't you think it would be wise to refresh our toilettes just a mite?" she added as they neared the main part of the manor.

"Isn't that Imogene being carried in?" Henrietta gasped as the huge entryway opened before them.

They dashed to the settee where the countess was being laid down.

"A vinaigrette, brandy, a wet cloth," Dunstan ordered as the three sisters hovered over her.

"My head may be split," Lady Imogene said clearly, although her eyes remained closed, "but there is no need to suffocate me. Brienne, speak to those . . . idiots. They claim they do not have Sarita." She forced her eyes open, but groaned and covered them with her hand.

"Where did you find Lady Ludlow?" the earl demanded, swinging his attention to the rough-clad young men who had carried her in.

The oldest was prodded forward by the red-faced lot. "Clem, he told us ta let no un pass," he stammered. "Well, her . . . her ladyship there was creepin' through them bushes 'n we didn't know it t'were her. When I grabbed her, she near bit me finger off. That's when I hit her. Didn't mean no harm. Me apologies, m'lady." He bobbed his head at the countess.

"I believe you, man, but wasn't there a young woman with her?" Dunstan demanded impatiently.

He shook his head and looked at the men behind him, who pled their ignorance with shrugs.

"She was right behind me." Lady Imogene struggled upright, hampered by three pair of helping hands. "She was."

"Perhaps the blow has befuddled you. Sarita must be in the gallery," the marchioness said uncertainly.

The countess opened her mouth to protest. It dropped further open as Lin Sullivan staggered into the hall.

"Deborah," he gasped. "Mandel swore he'd take Deborah. Where is she?"

"Enoch!" The happy cry turned their attention to the grand staircase at the far end of the entryway, where Deborah was struggling through the throng. In moments she raced down the steps and flew to Lin's open arms, sobbing with relief.

"Isn't Sarita with you?" Dunstan asked Reverend Durham, who had followed his daughter's steps.

"Why, no. She left some time ago with Lady Imogene."

"My God, Cris." Lin raised his face from the perfume of Deborah's golden hair, his joy mixed with his anguish. "Mandel must have meant Sarita. He told me this eve he was taking Miss Durham to France."

"Did you find his boat?" Dunstan swung to Jervy, who had followed Lin in.

"Aye, m'lord, and left the men with it."

"Where are the other men?"

"I sent one to find them. They should be together by now."

"Let's be away." The earl grabbed a pistol from the man beside him. He gripped Durham's shoulder. "I'll find her if I have to go to France, or I'll see Mandel in hell," he swore and was gone.

The tight gag cut into Sarita's mouth, bringing the salty taste of blood as Mandel held her before him in the saddle. She had had no chance to scream when he grabbed her from behind as she followed the countess.

Drawing his mount to a halt, Pierre untied the gag but did not free her hands. "Now *ma chérie*, that kiss." His lips closed on hers hungrily.

With all the will she possessed, Sarita forced herself to remain limp in his arms.

"Bah!" he spat. "The kiss of a fish." He spurred his mount forward, glancing to the rear to see if he was being pursued.

Frantic thoughts pulsed through Sarita's mind as they galloped along. *Surely they will know I am gone, know that Pierre has me,* she thought. But what if they don't know? Fear filled her, but her terror was forgotten as the steed stumbled, nearly unseating

Mandel and causing Sarita to tip precariously to one side.

Pierre let her fall to the ground and dismounted. Squatting by his mount, he ran his hand over the leg the horse refused to stand on, a string of French epithets bursting from him as he worked with the animal.

Hoping against hope, Sarita stumbled to her feet and began to run. In the dim light, brush and stones were hidden from sight, and she tripped, falling to the ground.

Tossing the saddlebags he carried to his shoulder, Mandel pulled her roughly to her feet. "Do not attempt that again, *ma chérie*." He twisted her arm painfully, pulling her forward, leaving the horse behind. "We are not far from the boat."

Moments later, Dunstan and Jervy reined in their lathered mounts, two of Pergrine's best, as Mandel's deserted steed hobbled away from them.

"He's headed straight for the boat, m'lord. 'Tain't too far. Much closer when mounted." Jervy's crooked teeth flashed in a wide grin.

Dunstan spurred forward. Minutes later Mandel heard the thudding hooves. Yanking Sarita along, he hurried his steps.

"Mandel!" Dunstan's voice broke over them as they came to the crest of a slope above the point where the boat lay. They could see Mandel's men huddled around it.

The Frenchman pushed Sarita aside, causing her to fall down the rocks, and fired his pistol at the earl.

The ball grazed the earl's horse, making it rear and plunge wildly about.

Running and jumping over the rocks, Mandel yelled at his men, who had scurried to push the boat into the Channel, to wait for him. One grabbed Mandel's arm and pulled him in as they struck the oars.

Forgetful of all but Sarita, Dunstan leapt from his horse and bounded over the rocks to her side. In one swift movement he lifted her from them and crushed her to him in relief.

Safe, Sarita's spirit revived. "Might it not be better, Cris, if you untied my hands?" her small voice broke through his thankful prayer.

Setting her down with a huge smile, he quickly undid the knotting.

Rubbing her wrists, Sarita turned to face him, her heart in her eyes.

"Thank God," he breathed and scooped her to him once more. Her arms twined about his neck as their lips met, all else forgotten.

"Not even a proper swoon," he teased as Jervy approached them, coughing loudly.

" 'Tisn't as bad as it might seem, m'lord," the little man said, pointing to the barely visible bobbing boat in the Channel. "Not that ye would notice." Jervy coughed again.

"Why didn't our men take action to prevent them from leaving?" Dunstan asked.

Jervy shook his head, then shrugged.

"We'll be happy with Finley and Pergrine," Dunstan said, his arm wrapped protectively about Sarita.

"They will never again give information to the enemy, and Gerard will have learned a hard lesson."

"M'lord," Jervy shifted his weight uneasily and tapped the earl's arm.

Dunstan paused as he leaned forward, intent upon kissing Sarita once more.

"Like as not them papers won't ever reach them French shores," Jervy grinned.

The earl peered questioningly from the small man to the boat on the water.

A deep chuckle broke from Jervy. "You see, m'lord, the men I left behind, they decided that the boat needed some repair . . . of a hinderin' nature. Those coves'll be swimmin' ashore soon enough," he added, waving towards the boat.

Slowly a grin, then a beaming smile, spread over Dunstan's features. "Repair, eh?" he repeated softly.

"Aye, m'lord."

The two broke into roaring laughter, but Sarita's joy turned to consternation, her warm heart became ice. The strange, begrimed little man seemed to know Cris well, and he had addressed him as m'lord.

Chapter XXIII

Three days after his rescue, his face still bearing the marks of his ordeal, but with a new, complete confidence, Lin Sullivan sat among the dowagers and the Durhams explaining what had been garnered from the constant stream of witnesses and government men that had poured in and out of the rectory's library since that turbulent night.

"All the men killed in this area during the past two years had stumbled across what Mandel was doing, or realized that Pergrine was involved," he said. "They were caught much as I," he added, referring to how he had strolled in the garden, been lured to the woods by a flickering light, and subsequently knocked senseless when the men he was spying on discovered him.

Deborah, sitting at Lin's side, shivered and tightened her hold on his arm.

"I was more fortunate than they." He smiled down at her and tenderly patted her hand.

Sitting across the solarium, Sarita smiled wanly at the pair's evident happiness, pushing back her own misery. Cris had yet to speak more than a greeting since their return to the rectory.

The solarium's door swung open. Lord Dunstan walked in, his face grim. "Jervy has just returned. They have captured the last man to leave the sinking boat, the last to see Mandel alive. We can be certain now, with this man's evidence, that the papers and documents as well as the gold are at the bottom of the Channel."

"And Mandel?" Lady Brienne asked.

"He was apparently attempting to swim to the French shore," Cris said, his skeptical look indicating his assessment of the man's chances.

The women, Lin, and Reverend Durham shook their heads, their relief that no new information had been received by the French tempered by the tragedy that the attempt had brought.

"What of Lord Pergrine and Mr. Finley?" Lady Phillippa asked softly.

"At worst, they face the hangman," Dunstan answered. "Lady Pergrine has gone to stay with her family. She never knew what her husband was about." He shook his head. "Lord Gerard has returned to London, a good deal chastened by all this. For now, the matter is essentially cleared. All the men involved are accounted for—either pulled from the Channel or caught after they came to land," the earl continued. "We've but a few more pages of testimony to complete for the War Ministry. Lin, could you come and help?" His eyes were on Sarita as he spoke, but she stared down at her hands tightly clenched in her lap.

"Of course. Bloody well glad to have this business finally done." Lin said, rising.

Reverend Durham also rose. "I must tell Monsieur Mandel the news about his son before he hears it from someone else," he said sadly.

"I will go with you, Father," Sarita said. "Let me

fetch my bonnet." She brushed past Dunstan without looking into his questioning eyes.

"I am sorry," Sarita said to Monsieur Mandel in front of the greenhouse. She had remained for a time after her father had left, helping the old Frenchman with his work as he doggedly carried on to cover his grief.

"There is nothing anyone can do, *mademoiselle.*" He shook his head slowly. "Pierre was always headstrong. He changed when the revolution struck, when we lost everything. He became violent. I thought that coming here would change that. I never understood. Perhaps if I had . . ."

"No, *monsieur,* you mustn't blame yourself," she entreated.

"I do not . . . most of the time. Do not worry," Monsieur Mandel sought to assure her.

"What will you do now . . . with Lord Pergrine gone?"

"Monsieur Sullivan . . . I mean Lord Dunstan. The change is *difficile* to remember, is it not?" The old man smiled wryly. "He called on me late last eve and told me he would sponsor my experiments. He assured me that others will be interested in my improvements in seed grains. *Je m'en tirerai*—I shall manage it. I have my plants . . . my flowers."

Sarita brushed his cheek with a kiss.

"*Merci, mademoiselle, merci,*" he mumbled, and shuffled into the greenhouse.

Sarita daubed at the tears which had come to her eyes. She knew that he had the courage to overcome this new sorrow, that his work would bring him hap-

247

piness once again. Slowly she turned and began the walk home. When she reached the thickest part of the woods, a square figure approached her.

"May I walk you to the rectory?" the earl's deep voice asked.

"I thought you had testimony to take," she accused.

"I left that to Lin. He is quite capable. May I?" Dunstan repeated softly.

"As you wish . . . my lord," she answered, walking past him, her eyes downcast.

They walked on in silence for many yards until Dunstan finally reached out, took her hand, and halted. With his other hand he forced Sarita to turn to him, and pressed her chin up. Their eyes met. He read the pain, the doubt, and the love in hers.

"I did not mean for you to learn the truth as you did," he began slowly. "I meant no harm. I did not know that first day I saw you that it would matter, that I would find my love, my life, here with you."

A large lump welled in Sarita's throat. "But why didn't you tell me later . . . that night in the woods?" She met his gaze searchingly.

"I felt that Lin's life depended upon no one knowing he was not the earl. I had endangered his life; I had to risk even our happiness to save him."

"But the dowagers knew." Her pain trembled in her voice. "And you have not spoken with me until now. Here alone."

Dunstan stiffened. "What can you have been thinking?" he asked in amazement. "Don't you see why I've been closeted with these men for the past three days? It had to be . . ." He paused. "I beg your under-

248

standing, your forgiveness, if you feel I have done wrong," he pleaded, his voice calm and earnest.

"Harden not your heart." Sarita had heard that passage often and now the words echoed in her mind. She studied the earl's features. Seeing the hope, the love, and the fear flickering over his face, her heart asked, *Why aren't you in his arms? Don't you love him? Haven't you avoided him these three days past? Isn't it your pride alone that has been injured?* A lone tear trailed down her cheek as the mist that had surrounded her heart and mind for the past three days evaporated. "I love you so," she choked out and rushed into his open arms.

Bright, joyous sunshine filtered through the stained-glass windows of Malvern Church in bright hues of red, green, blue, and yellow. Flowers of every kind, colour, and size, gathered from the fields and gardens as well as from Monsieur Mandel's greenhouse, had been placed in the windows and along the aisles.

Two brides stood before a proud and beaming Reverend Durham as they repeated the vows he pronounced over them.

In her mother's wedding gown of white and silver silk and lace, Sarita stood glowing with happiness, her burly Crispin beaming at her side; Deborah, a wisp of beauty in a gown of blue silk with pearls from Lady Phillippa, gazed lovingly at a proud and nervous Lin.

The vows completed, the rings placed on their fingers, Reverend Durham watched with a bursting heart as his daughters accepted their first kisses from their new husbands.

Then they were walking down the aisle into the church's age-old porch that had seen so many couples newly married. Well-wishers thronged about the tables laden with food and drink, which had been arranged beneath the large oak and in the gardens. Singing and cheering, a truly festive air reigned all day.

Later, as the last farewells were said and the coaches, brought from London by the earl, were driven to the front steps to collect the happy couples, a rousing cheer arose. In a trice they were gone.

"It was lovely, so lovely." Lady Phillippa daubed a tear away as the dowagers and the Durhams stood watching the dust billow in the coaches' wakes.

"Grandly done," Lady Imogene agreed with a sigh.

"Never thought I'd live to see him leg-shackled," Lady Henrietta beamed.

"Excellent young men, both of them," Reverend Durham solemnly pronounced.

The baroness alone stood to one side, having returned to her contankerous ways, her hauteur shielding her emotions.

"Brienne, surely you are pleased to see them wed," said the marchioness, putting an arm about the stiff shoulders.

The chin rose higher, quivering.

"You know they said their firstborn shall be named after you, be it boy or girl," Lady Imogene added, patting her on the back consolingly.

The baroness tightened her lips, a tear coursing down one cheek, then the other. "I was thinking of . . . of Robert, recalling our wedding day." Lady

Brienne's voice shook. "How happy we were. How brief our time seemed."

"Brienne, you've never let him go," Phillippa said, realizing for the first time the reason for the baroness's constant irritation and testy bouts. "All this time . . ."

"But don't you see?" Lady Henrietta took her sister's hand. "He is still with you. Isn't life memories—memories and tomorrows? Remembrances." She laughed gently. "No one can alter them or take them away." Her voice hardened. "Just as Crispin and Sarita, Deborah and Lin, have their tomorrows before them, we still have ours." Lady Henrietta laughed as the others gaped at her. "Think of the past few weeks, the past few days. Never have I had such experiences, such excitement, not such fear." She rolled her eyes.

Slowly Brienne extended her hand; the sisters formed a ring. "Will you travel with us, Henrietta?" she asked.

"Do you want me?" Lady Dunstan asked in surprise.

"Of course." The baroness smiled, her sisters echoing her. "After all, you are now the Dowager Countess of Dunstan." Everyone joined in her laughter.

Lord Dunstan looked down at his new wife nestled in his arms and smiled.

"What are you thinking?" Sarita asked at the mischievous glint in his eyes.

"About something you told me that night in the

woods. What were you doing that night?" He shifted his weight to get a better look at her features.

"Perhaps I should ask you the same," she quipped, then shook her head as he tried to answer. "How did you spend those three days I was avoiding you like the pox?" she asked, her mood changing.

"Arranging this," he said, waving his hand. "All the testimony I had to give was done then, all the reports written. I made certain no one and nothing could disturb us for the next month. And I arranged for the special license so that once I convinced you of my love we could be wed without delay."

A blush stole over Sarita's cheeks as passion flickered in his eyes, calling forth a like response in her own. "What are you thinking of?" she asked softly.

"It concerned Mother. . . . How you once said you would not envy Deborah for marrying Lord Enoch and having *his* mother as a mother-in-law," he reminded her, his eyes twinkling.

Sarita grabbed the pillow at her side and smashed it to her husband's head with all her might.

Laughing, he pulled it from her.

"Your mother was right. You are an incorrigible mischief maker," she retorted.

"What? An alliance against me already?" He leaned back against the coach seat, a hand across his brow. "What shall become of me. I must call the dowagers to rescue me."

"They know a hoax when they hear it . . . or see it," Sarita retorted, hard put to keep a straight face.

"But this is no sham," he said softly, drawing her

towards him. "None at all," he breathed as his lips claimed hers.

"This is the most excitement I have had since Lord Kennard proposed to me years ago," Lady Henrietta chattered animatedly as the dowagers walked down the rectory steps with Reverend and Mrs. Durham.

"You must be relieved to have us finally leave," Lady Brienne said, offering her hand.

" 'Tis a sad day to see such pleasant guests depart," the rector smiled sadly.

"There is much work to keep you from ever knowing we have gone. Your flock has returned." The baroness glanced to the group of people repairing the church roof. "There is also the purchaser of Lord Pergrine's lands to consider. The new owner will need guidance on how to correct all the injustices of the past few years." She grinned widely. "My nephew said they would be spending some months each year at the house. Of course we shall have to visit them . . . and you."

"There shall always be a warm welcome awaiting you," Mrs. Durham's quiet voice spoke as she took her husband's hand. "Thank you so much for the many conversations, the encouragement and guidance you have given. I had not realized the depth of my retreat from reality. I do believe all will be well now," she said, looking from the baroness to her husband with a new-found strength.

"I believe so, too," Lady Brienne nodded, "for everyone."

"Aren't you coming, Brienne?" Lady Imogene stuck her head out of the coach's window.

"Come along." Lady Phillippa waved a hand excitedly. "Who knows what lies before us."

"Bruises, with this coach," Lady Henrietta pronounced, thumping the horsehair squabs as the baroness joined them.

"Enough. We are not even off, and you are already complaining." Lady Brienne's stern features glared as she settled into the coach. Tapping the roof with her cane, she turned and waved farewell as Mr. Caine urged the teams forward. Her sternness faded as she looked at the three, each gazing questioningly from one to the other at her suddenly brusque manner. "I wouldn't want you to think I had changed too much, now would I?" she quipped.

Laughter burst from the three as she chuckled. As their laughter died away, a verse they had sung long ago burst from Lady Phillippa and was quickly taken up by the others.

Our minds to us kingdoms are,
Such present joys therein we find,
That it excels all other bliss
That earth affords or grows by kind:
Though much we want which most would have,
Yet still our minds forbid the crave.
Content to live, this is our stay;
We seek no more than may suffice;
We press to bear no haughty sway;
Look, what we lack our minds supply;
Lo, thus we triumph like queens,
Content with what our minds doth bring.*

* From "My Mind to Me a Kingdom Is" by Sir Edward Dyer (1550-1607).

Lady Brienne looked at her sisters as the song ended, a comfortable happiness easing her past cares. *Yes,* she thought, *we have our tomorrows.* A chuckle escaped her. *And what tomorrows they shall be!*

Love—the way you want it!

Candlelight Romances